ADIRA SHAMRA

A REBEL QUEEN

AF581458

RAM PRAKASH

Copyright © Ram Prakash
All Rights Reserved.

This book has been self-published with all reasonable efforts taken to make the material error-free by the author. No part of this book shall be used, reproduced in any manner whatsoever without written permission from the author, except in the case of brief quotations embodied in critical articles and reviews.

The Author of this book is solely responsible and liable for its content including but not limited to the views, representations, descriptions, statements, information, opinions and references ["Content"]. The Content of this book shall not constitute or be construed or deemed to reflect the opinion or expression of the Publisher or Editor. Neither the Publisher nor Editor endorse or approve the Content of this book or guarantee the reliability, accuracy or completeness of the Content published herein and do not make any representations or warranties of any kind, express or implied, including but not limited to the implied warranties of merchantability, fitness for a particular purpose. The Publisher and Editor shall not be liable whatsoever for any errors, omissions, whether such errors or omissions result from negligence, accident, or any other cause or claims for loss or damages of any kind, including without limitation, indirect or consequential loss or damage arising out of use, inability to use, or about the reliability, accuracy or sufficiency of the information contained in this book.

Made with ♥ on the Notion Press Platform
www.notionpress.com

Contents

Acknowledgements

First and foremost, I want to express my deepest gratitude to my father and mother, the reason I am here today. Your unwavering support and love have shaped the person I have become, and I owe it all to you.

To my friends and family, thank you for always standing by me, believing in me, and providing me with the encouragement I needed to keep going. Your faith in my abilities has meant the world to me.

I also want to extend my heartfelt appreciation to Karthick Mahendran, Senthill Irusa, Dinesh, Sudharshan, Shankar Nagarajan, Santhosh, prakash Samraj and our entire team. You all stood by me, believing in me at a time when I wasn't sure of myself. Together, you helped make this dream a reality.

A special thanks to Shruthi Bharadwaj, Shiva Priya, and Soundariya—each of you saw the writer in me before I even realized it myself. Your belief in my potential inspired me to pursue this journey with passion.

Finally, to Adiya—your handcrafted book, given to me before anyone else, was a special and cherished gift. Thank you for your support, which motivated me even more.

Once again, thank you to everyone who has supported me along the way. Your love, encouragement, and belief in me have made this book possible.

CHAPTER 1
The Silence Before the Storm

The air outside the palace was thick with tension. Shadows crept over the massive stone walls as the crowd pressed closer, eyes fixed on the towering gates. Inside, the battle had long since fallen silent, but no one knew what had transpired. Soldiers still clashed in pockets beyond the palace, the fight for freedom not yet complete. But here, at the heart of it all—nothing.

No one moved. No one spoke. The silence was deafening.

The people had come in the thousands, drawn by the promise of change, of an end to the terror that had ruled their lives for so long. But as the hours dragged on, unease began to take hold. Whispers spread like wildfire—was it over? Had they won? Or was it all for nothing?

For years, they had lived in fear, crushed beneath the weight of a tyrant's iron rule. He had stripped them of everything—hope, freedom, family. His name was a curse, spoken only in hushed tones. And now, as they stood waiting, doubt crept in. Could anyone truly defeat him?

A flicker of hope had brought them here, a small light in the darkness. But hope, they knew, could be easily extinguished.

From within the palace, there was no sign of what had happened. No word, no victory cry. Just silence.

And then, as the crowd strained to hear, a voice—faint, distant, yet unmistakable. It came from deep within the palace, barely audible through the heavy stone walls. A voice they all feared.

"I remember..." it began, slow and deliberate. The voice of a man who had held power for too long. A man who had never known defeat.

The crowd froze. The whispers died.

Inside the palace, the figure in the shadows shifted, his breath ragged, his body broken. But his will—unshaken. His name, the one that had haunted their nightmares for years, was now the last thing they feared.

Chancellor Dev.

CHAPTER 2
Rise of Dev

Dev wasn't always the tyrant who struck fear into the hearts of nations. He was once a prince, heir to a legacy of nobility and honor, the son of a ruler respected by his people. His father, the former Chancellor, governed with a balanced hand—strong, but fair, leading a kingdom where justice, though stern, prevailed. But in the world of power, honor is a fragile thing. Dev learned this the hard way.

He had grown up in the shadow of his father's greatness, expected to one day inherit the crown and lead with the same wisdom. But power is a dangerous game, and treachery festers where ambition lurks. The betrayal came from within, by those closest to the crown. His father's most trusted allies, the very ones who whispered counsel in his ear, plotted his downfall. They craved the throne, and when the time came, they struck—not with open blades, but with poison, lies, and deceit.

The coup was swift. His father's empire fell not in battle, but through manipulation, and as the kingdom collapsed around him, Dev watched the man he revered crumble, betrayed by those who had sworn loyalty. The rebellion was not fought on the battlefield but in dark chambers, where false promises and backstabbing brought his father to his knees.

It was in these moments of treachery that Dev's transformation began. Stripped of his innocence and trust, watching everything he knew burn to the ground, a darker realization dawned within him— **power was not given or inherited; it was taken** .

The fall of his father ignited something new in Dev. As the kingdom fractured and the throne lay vulnerable, the once hopeful prince shed the skin of idealism. He didn't seek to regain the throne for justice or for his father's legacy. No. Dev wanted vengeance—and more than that, he wanted absolute control. The betrayal had taught him that there was no room for weakness, no place for trust. He would not just rise to power—he would dominate .

Dev fought tooth and nail to reclaim the empire, but he did it on his own terms. Unlike his father, who ruled with honor and compassion, Dev had no interest in mercy or fairness. Each betrayal and every drop of blood spilled during the years of civil unrest only hardened his resolve.

Many believed they could manipulate Dev, thinking they could elevate him as a figurehead while pulling the strings from the shadows. They thought their cunning would make him a puppet king, easily controlled and easily discarded. They underestimated him.

With masterful precision, Dev played their game, appearing to accept their alliances while quietly laying the groundwork for his own rise. He fostered division among them, exploiting their egos and mistrust to create fractures in their once-unified front. As they celebrated their perceived victory, believing they had secured their power by controlling him, Dev revealed his true nature.

In a dramatic turn of events, he orchestrated a public display that shattered their illusions. One by one, he exposed their betrayals and ambitions, pitting them against one another in a ruthless game of power. The very alliances they thought would solidify their control became their undoing.

When the dust settled, it was clear who held the true power. Dev emerged not as a pawn, but as a master of the game, leaving behind a trail of broken ambitions and shattered loyalties. Those who once sought to manipulate him now faced his wrath, their plots unraveling as he demonstrated the true meaning of dominance. He reclaimed his throne, not just as a ruler but as a force of nature, solidifying his reign with the understanding that he would never again be a pawn in anyone's game.

When Dev finally claimed the throne, it was not as the heir of a noble chancellor—it was as a new kind of ruler. The boy who had watched his father's betrayal was gone, replaced by a man who had learned that trust was for fools, and mercy was for the weak. In his victory, a monster was born. The kingdom, once a place of honor, now became a fortress of fear.

From the ashes of his father's fall, Dev rose as the new Chancellor, but he was not the man his father had been. He had no interest in ruling for the good of the people. The crown was his, and now, his only goal was to keep it—at any cost. He trusted no one, saw allies as pawns, and ruled with an iron fist, ensuring that no one would ever have the power to betray him again.

Where his father had led through respect, Dev led through terror. His mind sharpened by betrayal, his heart hardened by years of struggle, he ruled with a cold ruthlessness. Any flicker of rebellion was extinguished before it could spark into flame. The people became nothing more than tools in his hands, their suffering merely collateral in his quest for ultimate control.

Chancellor Dev was born from betrayal, forged in the fires of power, and driven by the need to never fall as his father did. The kingdom would bend to his will, and he would ensure that no one, not even those closest to him, would ever rise against him. In his eyes, betrayal had given birth to the only truth that mattered—**power belonged to the ruthless** .

The Next Day...

Chancellor Dev wasted no time in cementing his reign with an iron grip. The moment he claimed the throne, he set his sights on those who had orchestrated his father's betrayal. One by one, he hunted them down, each act of retribution a brutal reminder of the price of treachery.

In a public square, where once his father had held courts of justice, Dev gathered the remaining conspirators—those who had whispered poison in his father's ear, those who had plotted in the shadows. He wanted the people to see. He wanted them to feel the weight of his wrath.

As the sun dipped low in the sky, casting an ominous glow over the crowd, Dev ordered their execution. The people watched in silence, their breaths caught in their throats. Each traitor was dragged before the gathered masses, fear etched into their faces as they realized the full extent of Dev's cruelty.

With a cold smile twisting his lips, Dev raised his hand, a signal for his guards. The first traitor, a once-respected advisor, was thrown to the ground. Dev stepped forward, his eyes burning with a fierce, dark light. "You thought betrayal would go unpunished?" he sneered, voice dripping with disdain. "This is the consequence of weakness."

Without hesitation, he raised his weapon—a gleaming blade that glinted wickedly in the fading light—and with one swift motion, he struck down the man who had dared to conspire against him. The crowd gasped, a collective intake of breath, but Dev's laughter echoed through the square, chilling them to the bone.

One by one, he executed each traitor, their pleas for mercy drowned out by the sound of steel on flesh. With every brutal death, he turned to the onlookers, his gaze sweeping across their terrified faces. The ruthlessness of his actions became a spectacle, a demonstration of power that resonated deep within their hearts.

As the last traitor fell, the square fell silent. The blood-stained ground was a stark reminder of the price of betrayal. Dev stood tall amidst the carnage, his chest swelling with a twisted sense of victory. He surveyed the crowd, his expression one of cruel satisfaction.

"Look at what happens to those who dare defy me!" he proclaimed, his voice booming. "This is your Chancellor—a man who fears no one and answers to no one! Kneel, and know that your lives depend on your loyalty!"

With that, the people, their hearts pounding with fear, dropped to their knees, trembling as they stared at the ground. They understood now that defiance would not be tolerated, that their Chancellor would not just rule but reign through terror.

Dev reveled in their submission, a wicked smile spreading across his face. He thrived on their fear, knowing it would keep them in line. In that moment, he transformed before their eyes—from a man seeking vengeance to a tyrant forged in ruthlessness. The laughter that escaped his lips was dark and greedy, a promise that he would not stop until every last whisper of dissent was silenced.

From that day forward, the people would know him not just as Chancellor, but as the monster he had become—one who would go to any lengths to secure his power, ensuring that no one would ever dare to rise against him again.

CHAPTER 3
After Sometime...

Adira, a 15-year-old, exuded charm and an unyielding spirit. She was a resolute fighter, steadfast in her convictions, and deeply engrossed in literature about revolutionary heroes. An astute student, she was particularly dedicated to her education.

One day, she was playing with a friend, forced to find hidden spots for their games to avoid the watchful eyes of the tyrannical ruler, Dev. He was a power-hungry and heartless chancellor, addicted to his authority and control.

In the midst of this grim reality, Adira and her friend stumbled upon a concealed group of rebels, secret activists of the revolutionary community. Unbeknownst to her, her own parents were part of this clandestine network, and soon, Adira would join their ranks. The stronger youths were recruited for training, preparing them for the impending battle against Chancellor Dev.

"Adira has always been a brave girl," Minervan, the leader of the community, remarked with admiration.

"Thank you," Adira replied with a determined spark in her eyes.

"How was your training today?" the leader inquired.

"It went well, . I'm eager to learn more about the art of combat to confront our formidable enemy," Adira said with fervor.

"That's the spirit, Adira. I know you'll get there, but for now, patience and practice are key," the leader assured.

In the world of our story, the children received fundamental training to safeguard themselves against potential threats from the enemy army. Among these youngsters, Adira stood out as the most enthusiastic and quick learner. Her insatiable curiosity drove her to master various skills, making her exceptional in archery and defense techniques, as well as martial arts. Her ability to grasp and adapt to new knowledge through keen observation was truly remarkable.

As the days passed, training became a routine, each one resembling the last. However, one fateful day, after the usual training session, Adira returned home only to witness a heart-wrenching and calamitous sight before her very eyes.

Adira's father devised a daring plan to target Arya's Wrath, the rumored vault believed to contain Chancellor Dev's vast wealth and weaponry. Yet, the vault's exact location remained a mystery, and many dismissed it as mere folklore. To turn this elusive goal into reality, he knew he needed more allies to join the fight.

Understanding that the first step was to inspire the people, he set his sights on a bold move—assassinating the town's head, a staunch supporter of Dev. This wasn't just about eliminating a single figure; it was a calculated strategy to ignite a fire of rebellion among the townsfolk. He believed that by striking down someone in power, he could create a ripple effect, stirring anger and resentment against the oppressive regime.

Adira's father envisioned a scene that would be impossible to ignore: the town's head, was a symbol of loyalty to Dev, suddenly brought low. The shock of the event would awaken the dormant courage in the hearts of the people. He hoped it would serve as a clarion call, urging them to rise up against the tyranny that had suffocated them for so long.

As he prepared for this dangerous undertaking, he felt a mix of fear and determination. The risks were immense, but he believed in the potential for change. He knew that true revolution required sacrifice, and he was ready to lead the charge, hoping that his actions would turn whispers of rebellion into a powerful, united force against Chancellor Dev.

Adira's father met with Minervan in a dimly lit room, the tension palpable as he laid out his bold plan. "We need to take down the town's head," he said urgently. "It's the first step to igniting a rebellion. We must show the people that we can fight back."

Minervan's brow furrowed in skepticism. "But how will that help us find Arya's Wrath? We still don't even know where the vault is."

"I know," Adira's father admitted, his voice steady. "But if we strike against the town's head, it will create a ripple effect. It'll show the people that change is possible, and it might draw out others who know where the vault is hidden."

Minervan paused, deep in thought. "You want to kill the town's head as a distraction? That's a huge risk. What if it backfires?"

"Believe me, Minervan. This is our chance," Adira's father replied, his eyes fierce with determination. "If we create enough chaos, we can rally the people behind us. They need a reason to rise, and this could be it. Once we have the support, we can dig deeper for the vault's location."

Minervan remained silent for a moment, weighing the gravity of the proposal. Finally, he nodded, the resolve settling in. "All right. If you believe this is the way forward, I'll stand with you. Let's make it happen."

With that agreement, a flicker of hope ignited between them, a shared commitment to take the first step in their fight against Chancellor Dev's tyranny.

But Dev was always one step ahead. His network of spies quickly caught wind of the brewing rebellion, and he saw this as an opportunity to tighten his grip on power. Instead of merely quashing the uprising, he devised a cunning plan to make an example of Adira's father and his group.

With a cold, calculating demeanor, Dev summoned his most brutal battalion—an elite force known for their merciless tactics. These soldiers thrived on fear and chaos, and he knew they would carry out his orders with ruthless efficiency. He instructed them to launch a swift and brutal attack, ensuring that the devastation would be swift and absolute.

As his soldiers prepared for the assault, Dev felt a twisted sense of satisfaction. He imagined the scene unfolding in the town—the sudden chaos, the terrified faces of the townspeople, and the swift, decisive action that would follow. He wanted everyone to see the price of rebellion; he wanted to drown any thoughts of defiance in blood.

When the attack began, it was like a storm unleashed. The brutal soldiers moved through the streets with a single-minded purpose, overwhelming Adira's father and his allies. The sounds of combat rang out, echoing through the town as people looked on in horror. Dev's soldiers struck swiftly, leaving no room for hope or resistance.

After Adira left the camp, one of the fellow men, Justin, approached the leader with concern. "Why did you make that decision? It's dangerous to send her away from us. I never expected this from you," Justin inquired.

As Adira departed from the scene, a mysterious figure suddenly emerged on the distant horizon. His face bore the unmistakable marks of distress, hinting at urgent news concealed within his anxious demeanour. With a sense of urgency, he proclaimed, "Adira's parents have been apprehended by the soldiers, all due to her father's shadowy ties to the revolutionary community."

The leader, gripped by deep concern, questioned, "How did this dramatic turn of events come about?"

The informant responded, "It all traces back to Rishab, a fellow member of our clandestine group, responsible for brokering deals with various factions. He has been captured by the relentless soldiers, and his connection to Adira's parents became the catalyst for their arrest."

In a tense moment, Justin, his eyes filled with determination, declared, "We must take immediate action to safeguard this family, especially Adira."

The leader contemplated for a moment before responding, "Hmm... If we were to keep her here, it would confirm to her parents that they belong to our activist community. They'd also realize that we're training children. If they come searching for her, it could jeopardize our entire community."

Justin protested, "So, you're willing to risk a child's life for that?"

The leader responded, "I know you're resolute, but this is not the time. The sun will rise, and their downfall will be because of her. The day will come when they'll pay for their actions, but for now, exercise patience."

The leader acknowledged the difficulty of the decision but remained resolute, "I understand it's a hard choice, but we've already lost many lives. You may worry about one child, but I'm concerned for her parents. I know her well, and I believe she'll survive out there. When she returns, she'll be prepared for the struggle. Mark my words, she will bring an end to their leadership."

Adira and Vihan strolled back to her home. As they approached, a distressing sight met their eyes: Adira's parents were bound, and soldiers were subjecting them to a brutal beating. The surge of anger within Adira intensified, but she clung to the leader's words, acting as though she were innocent. She rushed toward her parents, determined to intervene.

The soldiers halted her progress, their stern voices demanding, "Who are you?" asked Soldier 1.

Her father responded, "She is my daughter."

With suspicion in their eyes, the soldiers asked in unison, "Are you part of that activist community?"

Her father replied firmly, "No, she knows nothing about that."

Soldier 1 lost his temper, striking her father across the face. "I didn't ask you to.. be quiet.. Answer me! Are you connected to this community?" he demanded.

Following the leader's guidance, Adira maintained her facade of calm innocence. "No, I don't know anything about that," she replied.

Soldier 1 nodded, seemingly convinced, and remarked, "Yeah, that's right. She's just a young and fragile girl. What could she possibly do?"

The soldiers shared a cynical laugh, unaware of the fire burning fiercely within Adira, as she concealed her true emotions.

(with that laugh **soldier1** leaned slightly towards the adira's neck and kissed in her neck and tried to hug her....)

Adira's father stepped in and uttered, "You fool, you're an absolute imbecile. Release my child. I am the one you're looking for. If you intend to inflict harm, direct it towards me. Remove your hands from my child."

Soldier 1 responded with anger, "You wretched, uncivilized imbecile! You dare to command me?" He delivered a fierce punch to her father's face, causing him to scream in agony.

The soldier raised his gun, aiming it squarely at Adira's father. The world seemed to hold its breath, the cold steel of the weapon gleaming in the dim light. The soldier's twisted grin made it clear—this was an execution.

In that heartbeat, something snapped inside Adira. A surge of raw fury flooded her veins, driving her into motion. Without thinking, she lunged forward, her movements swift and fierce. Her hand clamped down on the soldier's wrist like a vice, twisting it sharply. His grip faltered, and the gun slipped from his hand, clattering to the ground.

The soldier's eyes widened, shock rippling across his face as he struggled to comprehend what had just happened. But Adira gave him no time. In one fluid motion, she scooped up the fallen weapon, the familiar weight solid in her hands.

Without hesitation, she spun on her heel, leveling the barrel at the first soldier's chest. Her finger tightened on the trigger. Bang! The shot cracked through the air, a clean, perfect hit. The soldier crumpled to the ground, dead before his body hit the dirt.

The second soldier, just a few feet away, fumbled for his own gun, panic in his eyes. He wasn't fast enough. Adira was already moving, her gaze locking onto him like a predator zeroing in on prey. Another shot fired— bang! —and the second soldier dropped, his weapon still half-drawn, never having a chance.

The entire exchange lasted mere seconds, but the weight of it hung heavy in the air. The battlefield fell silent, the bodies of the soldiers lying still at Adira's feet. She stood there, chest heaving, the gun still warm in her hand, her heart racing with the thrill of survival.

Her father stared at her, eyes wide with a mixture of shock and awe. He had just witnessed the full force of what his daughter was capable of. Adira met his gaze, her face hardened, the fire inside her still burning bright.

This wasn't just a fight for survival—it was a glimpse of what she was becoming.

Other soldiers who had witnessed this alarming turn of events closed in, moving to apprehend her. Among them, Soldier 3, known as Rizwan, took aim at Adira and discharged his weapon.

However, Adira's mother intervened, and another soldier continuously fired, with her parents bravely shielding her from the hail of bullets. They stood like an unyielding fortress, protecting their daughter.

Adira stood drenched in her parents‘ blood, witnessing their tragic demise. As the crowd gathered to protect her, the situation quickly escalated into a riot.

"Look at that, a young child has the courage to seek revenge on these oppressors while the rest of us remain passive spectators," cried out voices in the crowd.

In the midst of the chaos, many lost their lives and sustained injuries. Yet, a newfound spirit of courage emerged, and little did anyone know that a fierce-hearted leader had been born. Adira, her heart ablaze with anger and determination, her eyes blazing with intensity.

Someone from the soldier group used a walkie-talkie to urgently signal the superiors , "The nearby team is on their way...,"replied from the superior in walkie-talkie . In the midst of these chaotic moments, the people rallied to safeguard Adira and protect her from further harm.

After the chaos of the riot had subsided, the frightened crowd sought refuge deep within the nearby forest. As they huddled together, tension filled the air, and discussions about the tumultuous incident unfolded. Meanwhile, the soldiers, fueled by relentless determination, scoured the area, their primary mission being the relentless pursuit of a young girl named Adira. They left no stone unturned, even going as far as intruding into the homes of innocent people.

Rathore, one of the individuals gathered in the forest, voiced his concerns, "For the time being, we find solace in the shelter of these woods, but it won't be long before they apprehend us."

"What's our next move?" another member of the group inquired.

Rathore contemplated the question, his gaze filled with determination. "We must take the next step, whatever that may entail."

Vikram, another member of the group, sought clarification, "What do you mean by 'the next step'?"

"We must decide our course of action," Rathore replied. "In some way, we have unwittingly ignited this conflict. Now we must choose to either stand and fight or accept our fate."

Vikram's voice quivered with frustration, "Are we really willing to risk our lives for the sake of one small girl?"

Rathore's expression remained resolute as he answered, "For the sake of a single young girl, our resolve will be put to the ultimate test."

Dev sat in his grand chamber, surrounded by advisors, when a messenger rushed in, panting and drenched in sweat. The news delivered was not what Dev had expected. His face, calm at first, slowly contorted with disbelief and fury.

"A single girl...?" Dev muttered, his voice barely containing the rising storm within him. "A single girl has undone my plans?" He rose from his chair, pacing with clenched fists. "How can this be? How could one young woman spark a rebellion, make fools of my soldiers, and turn my people against me?"

He slammed his fist onto the table, the sound echoing through the room. His eyes burned with rage. "The people... they are nothing but sheep! Mindless! They exist to follow me, to be molded by my will. She... she's poisoned them with hope.

And hope," his voice dropped into a low growl, "is the most dangerous weapon of all."

Dev paused, his expression darkening with a twisted determination. "I must crush this spark before it becomes a fire. She must be found—arrested, dragged through the streets so the people can see what happens when they dare challenge me."

He turned sharply to his generals. "Make no mistake, we will not simply arrest her. I want her broken. Torture her until she begs for mercy, until her spirit is nothing but dust beneath my feet. Let the people witness her suffering and understand—no one defies me. No one."

His generals nodded, but Dev's eyes stayed fixed on the far wall, as if already envisioning the brutal spectacle he would create. "I will kill hope itself."

As news of Adira's uprising spread, the once-silent streets of the town buzzed with a mix of awe and fear. People gathered in hushed whispers, some dumbfounded by the audacity of the young woman who had dared to defy Dev, while others trembled at the inevitable consequences. Adira's defiance had sparked a flame of hope, but it was a flickering flame that could be snuffed out just as easily as it had been lit. The people were afraid. They had seen what happened to those who opposed the chancellor's iron rule.

Eyes darted nervously as rumors began circulating: Dev had ordered a brutal retaliation. He wouldn't just punish Adira—he would send a message. It was his way of crushing any seeds of rebellion before they could grow into a forest of resistance.

Meanwhile, inside Dev's grand chamber, the ruthless chancellor gave the final order, his face contorted in a mask of cold fury. “Kill every single one of them,” he commanded, referring to the rebels who had stood beside Adira. “Make sure she watches. And then...” his voice dropped, chilling his generals to their bones, “send her to the torture chambers. Let her rot among the broken bodies of those who thought they could fight me.”

Dev's generals nodded grimly, knowing all too well what awaited in the torture chambers. A place where the walls echoed with the cries of those who had dared to defy his rule. For months, years even, he had dragged rebels and dissidents into the public square and executed them, a constant reminder of his power. It was not enough to kill them—Dev made sure their deaths were slow and agonizing, a spectacle for the masses.

The people, even now, could sense what was coming. Fear gripped their hearts as they imagined the worst. Would it be their fathers next? Their sons? Their daughters? Some cowered in their homes, while others, conflicted and confused, felt a surge of hope they didn't fully understand. Yet, that hope was weighed down by the terror of what Dev would do next.

As Dev's brutal order swept through the town, soldiers stormed into homes, dragging out anyone even remotely connected to the rebellion. The ground beneath the people's feet seemed to tremble as Dev prepared to demonstrate once more that no one could stand against him and live. This time, though, there was something different in the air—a tension, a faint resistance that even the strongest fear couldn't entirely suffocate.

But Dev, in his arrogance, believed he could crush this hope just like the others. His brutality was not just for Adira, but for everyone. He would make sure the entire town watched as he reminded them of his unchallenged power, snuffing out any chance of rebellion before it could fully ignite.

In the quiet of the hidden camp, the weight of Adira's earlier actions hung heavy in the air. The young girl who had barely begun to understand the depth of her own strength had unknowingly ignited a flame that could no longer be contained. It was the fire of rebellion, sparked by the moment she had fought back, not just against the soldiers who had taken her parents' lives, but against the very system that allowed such atrocities to happen.

Word of Adira's defiance had spread like wildfire, faster than anyone could have anticipated. The story of how she had disarmed and killed the soldier who murdered her parents had reached every corner of the oppressed villages. Her bravery was whispered about in hushed tones, a symbol of the hope that still flickered in the hearts of the people—hope that had once been crushed under the iron rule of Dev's tyranny.

But now, that hope had begun to rise.

Inside the camp, tension gripped the rebels who gathered around Minervan, their supposed leader. The atmosphere was thick with fear and uncertainty as news of Dev's brutal retaliation reached them. The rebels had no idea what to do next, and the weight of that indecision was suffocating. They argued among themselves, desperate to find a way out, desperate to hold onto the fragile hope that Adira's actions had sparked.

"How much longer can we hide?" one of the rebels yelled, his voice filled with frustration. "We may have given people a reason to believe, but look at what's happening! Dev's army is hunting us down, and he's slaughtering anyone who stands with us."

Another rebel, his hands trembling, added, "We're just a handful of fighters! Dev's soldiers will find us, and when they do, it will be the end."

Minervan, standing at the head of the gathering, watched them all with a calm that now seemed unnatural. He had led them to this point, guided them through the chaos, but now he was strangely silent. His mind churned with thoughts far removed from the argument around him.

Adira, the symbol of their resistance, stood nearby, still bloodied from her earlier fight, her eyes distant. She was no longer the scared girl who had watched her parents die; she had become something else entirely. But even she couldn't ignore the fear that now gripped the camp—the fear that maybe, just maybe, their fight had only led to more suffering.

Minervan finally spoke, his voice soft but firm. "We're at a crossroads. Yes, we've lost people. Yes, Dev's army is brutal. But what choice do we have? We either stay hidden like cowards or we fight. We've come this far, and now we have something we didn't have before—hope."

His words were calculated, designed to keep the rebels from falling apart, but underneath that speech was something darker. Minervan knew what was coming. He had ensured it. As much as the rebellion had begun to ignite, he had always intended to extinguish it in one swift motion, ensuring his own survival in Dev's regime

Outside, as the night grew darker, the forest stirred with unseen danger. Dev's soldiers, armed and ready, began their quiet advance toward the hidden camp. Minervan had led them here, all in secret, ensuring that every detail of the rebels' hiding place was known to the enemy. His betrayal was not born out of fear, but out of ambition. For Minervan, there was no future in rebellion, only in power—and he intended to seize it.

The camp's guards, unprepared for such an assault, were taken out quickly, their bodies falling silent into the underbrush. The soldiers moved like shadows, surrounding the camp, their swords ready, their orders clear: capture those who resisted, slaughter those who fought back, and most importantly, bring Adira to Dev, alive.

The hidden camp, once a sanctuary, had erupted into chaos. The night sky, veiled in darkness, was suddenly alive with the shouts of battle and the clash of steel. Dev's soldiers, moving with ruthless precision, descended upon the unsuspecting rebels like a pack of ravenous wolves, cutting down anyone who dared stand in their way. They had come under the cover of night, swift and silent, and by the time the alarm was raised, it was already too late.

Adira, still bruised and bloody from her earlier battle, barely had time to process what was happening before the camp was under siege. Grabbing a discarded blade, she charged into the fray, a fire blazing in her eyes. Despite her wounds, she fought with the fury of someone who had nothing left to lose. Her body moved with a fluidity born of desperation, each strike calculated, each blow intended to take down as many of Dev's soldiers as possible.

But they were too many.

For every soldier she felled, two more took their place. The rebels, though brave, were no match for Dev's well-trained forces. Men and women screamed as they were cut down, their bodies falling lifelessly to the ground. The camp, once filled with the hope of rebellion, was now drenched in blood and despair.

In the midst of this carnage, Minervan stood back, his face expressionless as he watched the slaughter unfold. His betrayal, the price of his own ambition, was complete. He had sold out the rebellion, leading Dev's forces straight to the camp in exchange for power and safety. Now, as the bodies of his former comrades littered the ground, he felt no remorse—only satisfaction.

The captain of Dev's army approached him, his sword dripping with blood. "Is the girl still alive?" he asked, his voice cold and detached.

Minervan nodded, his eyes narrowing. "She's still fighting."

The captain glanced toward the chaos, where Adira's figure could be seen moving through the battlefield, her blade flashing in the moonlight. "Good," he said, his voice laced with cruelty. "Dev wants her alive."

Minervan smirked. "She'll wish she wasn't."

As Adira fought on, her breath ragged and her body aching from the effort, she felt the weight of inevitability pressing down on her. Her comrades were falling all around her, the fight draining from their bodies as they were overwhelmed. Even her own movements were slowing, the strength leaving her arms as the sheer number of enemies closed in.

And then, with a sickening thud, the hilt of a sword struck the back of her head. She stumbled, dropping to her knees, her vision swimming as the world tilted around her. The blade she had been clutching fell from her hand, clattering uselessly to the ground. Before she could react, rough hands grabbed her arms, forcing them behind her back as soldiers bound her wrists with thick rope.

"No!" she screamed, struggling against them with all her might. But it was no use. The soldiers lifted her to her feet, dragging her through the camp as her fellow rebels looked on in helpless despair.

At the center of the camp, the captain of Dev's forces stood waiting, his cold eyes fixed on Adira as she was brought before him. He studied her with the same indifference one might show an insect before crushing it underfoot.

"Bind her," he ordered.

The soldiers forced Adira to her knees, her face pressed into the dirt as they tied her legs together. Blood trickled from a cut on her head, mixing with the grime beneath her. But even as she knelt there, bruised and broken, her eyes burned with defiance.

"You think this will break me?" she said, her voice low but unshaken, dripping with contempt.

"You think Dev can destroy the hope we've ignited?"

The captain sneered, his lips curling in amusement. "Hope? There is no hope here. Only death."

With a swift motion, he signaled to his men. The soldiers, with mechanical precision, dragged the surviving rebels—those who hadn't been slaughtered in the initial assault—into the center of the camp. Adira's heart sank as she watched them line up her comrades, their faces bruised and bloodied, their eyes filled with fear.

"What are you doing?" she demanded, her voice hoarse.

The captain leaned down, his face mere inches from hers, his breath hot and foul. "Do you know what Dev wants, Adira?" His voice was low, laced with cruel intent. "He wants to send a message."

He grabbed her chin, forcing her to look up at him. "To everyone who dares to defy him, this will be their fate." His eyes glinted with malice as he tightened his grip, his voice growing darker. "They will be broken, humiliated, and punished... to death."

His words hung in the air like a dark promise, the threat of Dev's wrath bearing down on her like a weight. Yet, even as he delivered this grim proclamation, the fire in Adira's eyes refused to die

In the town square, under the pale glow of dawn, the people gathered in trembling silence. Word had spread of the rebellion's crushing defeat, and now, they stood in horror, waiting for the inevitable display of Dev's brutality. Soldiers had forced them into the square, their faces drawn and fearful, as Dev's orders echoed through the streets.

Adira and the remaining rebels were dragged to the center of the square, their hands bound, their bodies beaten. The people gasped as they saw her, the young girl who had sparked their hope now paraded before them like a trophy. Dev's soldiers shoved her to the ground, her knees hitting the cobblestones with a sickening thud.

And then, Dev himself appeared.

He strode into the square, his face twisted into a mask of cold, unfeeling cruelty. He was dressed in his finest robes, the very image of power and dominance. As he approached the center of the square, the crowd parted in fear, not daring to meet his gaze.

"Look at them," Dev snarled, his voice echoing through the square. "These are the ones who dared to stand against me. These are the fools who thought they could bring hope to a world I control."

He gestured toward the rebels, his lips curling in disgust. "Hope is a lie. Hope is weakness. And I will show you what happens to those who spread it."

With a nod, he signaled his men. The soldiers grabbed one of the rebels—a young man barely old enough to fight—and dragged him forward. Without hesitation, one of the soldiers raised his sword and brought it down in a swift, brutal strike.

The crowd gasped as the rebel's body crumpled to the ground, lifeless. Blood pooled at Dev's feet, but his expression remained cold, unfeeling.

"This," Dev continued, "is what happens to those who defy me. There is no mercy. No leniency. Only death."

The people stood frozen, their hearts filled with terror as they watched the brutal display of power. Some looked away, unable to bear the sight, while others wept silently, knowing that they could be next.

But amidst the horror, Adira refused to break. Even as her comrades were struck down one by one, she kept her head high, her eyes filled with defiance. She knew that Dev wanted her to beg for mercy, to break under the weight of his cruelty. But she wouldn't give him the satisfaction.

As the executions continued, Dev turned his attention to Adira. "And now, for the one who dared to spark this fire," he said, his voice dripping with malice. "The girl who thought she could challenge me."

He stepped toward her, towering over her kneeling form. "You've cost me a great deal, child. Your little rebellion has caused quite a stir. But don't think for a second that you've won. I will crush every last ember of hope you've ignited."

He bent down, his face inches from hers. "And when I'm done with you, the people will know that defying me only leads to suffering."

With a sharp nod, he gave the order. The soldiers grabbed Adira and dragged her toward the torture chamber—Dev's infamous lair of agony, where those who dared to resist his rule were broken, body and spirit.

But even as she was dragged away, Adira's spirit remained unbroken. She knew that Dev's power was built on fear, and fear alone. And though she had been captured, she had given the people something Dev couldn't take away—a reason to fight.

As Dev's voice boomed through the town square, the people stood in stunned silence. But deep within their hearts, the seed of rebellion had already taken root. And though they feared what was to come, they knew that Dev's reign would not last forever.

Because hope, once sparked, was impossible to extinguish.

CHAPTER 4
Rise of a new Hope...

Vihan stood on the outskirts of the crumbling city, watching in horror as Adira was dragged through the streets, her once-strong frame beaten and bound by Dev's soldiers. The girl who had ignited a spark of hope among the people was now at the mercy of the tyrant who ruled with fear and cruelty. Vihan's fists clenched, his heart heavy with both anger and helplessness. He had lost everything in that same battle—his family, his home, and now, it seemed, Adira was slipping away too.

As the sun set over the bloodstained streets, Vihan's mind swirled with thoughts of revenge and despair. He wanted to charge in, to save Adira, to make things right, but he knew it was impossible. He was just one man—broken, lost, and unsure of how to fight back against the overwhelming power of Dev's forces.

Suddenly, a voice called out to him from behind.

"You can't win this battle alone," the voice said with a calm authority.

Vihan turned to see a tall, imposing man stepping out of the shadows. His face was hardened from years of battle, his eyes sharp with wisdom and determination. It was Kate Nilan, the leader of a hidden resistance group that had been quietly waging war against Dev's regime.

Kate was known to be ruthless in battle, a man who had survived countless wars, and yet his gaze held something different now—something that cut through Vihan's despair.

"I've been watching you," Kate said. "You're not the only one who's lost everything. But if you want to make a difference, you can't do it like this. Come with me. I'll show you how to fight back. The right way."

Vihan, still trembling from his emotions, hesitated. But there was something about Kate's presence—his words—that gave him a sense of direction he hadn't felt since the day his world was shattered.

Weeks passed, and Vihan found himself deep in the mountains, training under Kate's strict but effective mentorship. Kate wasn't just a soldier; he was a strategist, a man who understood the intricacies of warfare and survival. Vihan learned how to fight, how to shoot, and how to move like a ghost through enemy lines. Every day, as he honed his skills, the image of Adira in chains burned in his mind, fueling his desire for revenge.

It wasn't long before Vihan rose in the ranks of Kate's hidden group. He was no longer the lost, broken man he had been. He was a warrior, with a clear purpose: to end Dev's reign of terror and to avenge the death of his family.

One night, after a grueling training session, Vihan received news that left him stunned. Kate's informants had intercepted a message revealing the truth about Minervan—the man who had once stood with them in the resistance. It was Minervan who had betrayed them, selling out their cause for power. He had taken control of the town, manipulating Dev's fear tactics to maintain his authority. And even worse, he was the one responsible for the death of Adira's father.

Vihan's rage simmered beneath the surface. He had always known there was something off about Minervan, but to find out that he had betrayed them all for his own selfish gain—it was almost too much to bear.

But the news that came next shook him to his core.

Adira had killed Minervan.

The story was almost too unbelievable, but it had come from multiple sources. Despite being imprisoned in Dev's brutal torture chamber, Adira had not broken. In fact, she had become a symbol of resistance for the other prisoners, inspiring them to fight back, even in their darkest hour.

According to the reports, Minervan had been overseeing the torture, arrogant in his newfound power, but Adira had found a way to fight back. In a stunning act of defiance, she had used a small rod, one she had scavenged from the prison's floor, to brutally beat Minervan to death. His screams had echoed through the chamber, and when the guards finally arrived, they found Adira standing over his lifeless body, her face etched with determination.

The story of Adira's defiance spread quickly through the underground networks, and once again, she became a beacon of hope. Even in the darkest corner of Dev's empire, she had shown that tyranny could be fought, that no matter how powerful their enemies seemed, they could still bleed.

But as her legend grew, so did Dev's paranoia. Under the cover of night, Adira was transferred to an unknown location, whisked away to a secret chamber far from any prying eyes. Dev's army took every measure to ensure her whereabouts remained a mystery, guarding the location with the utmost secrecy. Even those within the highest ranks didn't know where she was held.

To the outside world, Adira vanished. Rumors swirled in the resistance camps, some claiming she had been executed, others believing she had escaped. But no one truly knew. Her absence left an eerie silence, but her defiance still lingered in the hearts of the people, a spark waiting for the right moment to ignite into something unstoppable. Even locked away in the shadows of Dev's empire, Adira's spirit refused to be extinguished.

Vihan stood at the edge of the camp, staring out into the distance. The weight of everything that had happened pressed down on him, but this time, he didn't feel lost. Adira's courage had reignited something in him. She had done what no one else could—she had taken down Minervan, the traitor, and ignited hope once again. And now, Vihan knew his fight wasn't over.

With Kate's group behind him and Adira's spirit driving him forward, he was ready to face whatever came next. Dev's cruelty had taken everything from him, but now he had a purpose. He would avenge his family, fight for the people who still suffered under Dev's iron rule, and ensure that Adira's sacrifice wouldn't be in vain.

The battle was far from over, and Vihan was ready to join the fight, stronger than ever.

Vihan, fueled by an unwavering determination and the pain of his personal losses, scoured the land in search of Adira. Every step he took was a step closer to confronting the man who had taken everything from him—Dev. Alongside Kate and the hidden resistance team, Vihan worked tirelessly to aid those who were suffering under Dev's oppressive rule. Quietly, they helped families escape from the brutality, smuggling resources and information that could weaken Dev's iron grip.

CHAPTER 5
After FEW Years...

Vihan, with Kate's leadership, began organizing secret revolutionary camps. These camps became training grounds where ordinary citizens transformed into warriors, preparing themselves for the inevitable clash against the regime. They practiced stealth attacks, learned how to use weapons, and studied tactics for guerrilla warfare. Vihan emerged as a vital figure in these camps, channeling his rage into empowering others, all while keeping his ultimate goal in mind—rescuing Adira and ensuring Dev's fall.

Whispers spread through the camps of a looming confrontation. Kate's team, hardened and ready after months of covert preparation, knew the time was nearing. Vihan, now a key leader among them, gave hope to those ready to risk it all. But amidst this growing revolution, a sense of urgency gnawed at him. He had to find Adira before it was too late, before Dev crushed all hope.

As they drew closer to the day of reckoning, Dev's forces intensified their patrols. Tensions grew. Every night, Vihan looked into the eyes of the fighters he had trained and knew the weight of their expectations. But he kept his focus sharp—Dev's reign of terror would soon crumble, and Adira would be at his side to witness it. The final pieces were falling into place, and Vihan knew that when the moment came, their revolution would either rise or fall in the shadow of Dev's downfall.

The next scene would see Vihan and his comrades on the brink of action, the tipping point that would ignite their long-awaited revolution.

Vihan stood alone in the shadowed alleyway, his breath shallow, heart thundering in his chest. The city's cold night air seemed to cling to him, as if the weight of the truth he'd just learned had made everything heavier, more oppressive. For years, he had been chasing shadows, gathering whispers, piecing together fragments of hope. But tonight, everything changed.

He hadn't been expecting the informant—an insider, a mole within Dev's ranks—who had risked everything to meet him. The man had approached with caution, his face hidden beneath a hood, voice low and wary. Vihan had almost dismissed him, thinking it was another false lead, another cruel game played by Dev's regime to mislead and manipulate the resistance.

But the words the spy whispered had shattered Vihan's world: ***Adira is alive.***

His pulse had quickened, every muscle tensing, but the spy wasn't done. He revealed more—the brutal truth of her imprisonment, locked away in one of Dev's secret torture chambers, hidden deep within the empire. It was a place where hope was meant to die, where the strongest wills were broken, and from which no one was ever meant to return.

Vihan staggered backward, the revelation hitting him like a blow to the gut. His years of searching, his sleepless nights and desperate plans—none of them had brought him this close. Adira, the woman who had become a symbol of hope for their people, was alive but enduring unimaginable torment. And the worst part? Dev was keeping her imprisonment a closely guarded secret, using her suffering as leverage, her defiance twisted into a silent message: *Even your strongest will break.*

The spy's eyes were dark, filled with a quiet fear. "Dev knows the power she holds. He's hiding her not to protect her, but to keep her spirit from inspiring more rebellion."

As the spy vanished back into the shadows, Vihan remained rooted to the spot, his mind reeling. Adira was alive. The knowledge flooded him with a mix of anguish and fury. She had been suffering while he had been out here, fighting, searching, believing she was lost forever.

But now he had a chance. He knew where she was. He could finally do what he'd failed to do for so long—bring her back. Free her.

Vihan's hands tightened into fists, the weight of the truth pressing down on him like a storm. His mind raced, yet one thing crystallized above all else: this wasn't just about rescuing Adira anymore. This was about striking at the heart of Dev's regime, about freeing the symbol of resistance and proving to the people that even in the darkest corners of Dev's empire, hope could not be crushed. It was a chance to reignite the fire that had been smoldering for so long.

He had spent countless nights imagining this moment, dreaming of how it would feel to finally find her. In those dreams, he had pictured a triumphant reunion—standing side by side, as equals, ready to lead the final charge against Dev. But reality was far crueler. Now, all he could think about was the suffering she had endured, trapped in one of Dev's most vile torture chambers. The thought of her, broken and alone for years, twisted his insides with guilt.

Adira, once the fierce symbol of defiance and hope, reduced to a mere ghost in Dev's hellish prison. The girl who had inspired thousands, who had stood fearless against tyranny, had been enduring torment all this time—and he hadn't been there to protect her. The guilt felt suffocating, clawing at his chest with every breath.

Where were you when she needed you most? The question echoed relentlessly in his mind. He had failed her, not just as a comrade, but as the one person who had vowed to never leave her side. It was unbearable, the weight of it gnawing at him, but it also fueled his determination. He wouldn't let her be lost to Dev's cruelty.

Vihan forced himself to move, slipping out of the shadows and into the dimly lit streets, the enormity of the task ahead sharpening his focus. He couldn't afford hesitation or doubt now. He knew what he had to do.

He made his way toward the safehouse where his comrades were waiting. Each step felt heavier than the last, but beneath the crushing guilt was a searing resolve. This rescue would not only be for Adira—it would be for the people. For every family Dev had shattered, every life his regime had destroyed. Adira's rescue would send a message that no prison, no amount of torture, could break the spirit of rebellion.

As he approached the entrance to the safehouse, his mind cleared. The plan was forming—solid, relentless, fueled by the urgency of her situation. He would find her, free her, and together they would do what they had always set out to do: bring down Dev's empire.

But there was one final thought that gripped him as he reached the door: *What will I find when I see her again?* The girl he had once known might be gone, replaced by someone who had suffered unimaginable horrors. He wasn't prepared for that, but it didn't matter. He couldn't fail her again.

The revolution would begin with her freedom. And no matter what it took, he would tear through Dev's regime to make sure of it.

He clenched his fists, his mind swirling with conflicting emotions. His first instinct was to run to Kate, to tell him everything. But something stopped him. Doubt. Fear. He didn't know if Kate would even help. The leader of their rebel group had grown more cautious over the years, more strategic. Would he risk everything for one person, even if that person was Adira?

Adira...

Her name echoed in his mind, bringing with it a flood of memories—memories that Vihan had held onto like a lifeline. He could see her so clearly in his mind: the way her eyes burned with fierce determination, the way her laughter had once echoed in the streets of their village. She had been more than just a friend—she had been his beacon of hope, his guiding light. Even now, in her absence, she was the reason he fought, the reason he had never given up.

He remembered their childhood, when they would race through the fields, carefree and full of dreams. Back then, nothing had seemed impossible. Adira had always been the brave one, the one who believed in something greater, even before the rebellion. She was the one who had ignited the fire in him, who had convinced him that they could fight back, that they could make a difference.

Vihan let out a shaky breath, his chest tightening as the memories flooded back. He couldn't lose her. Not like this. She had been the heart of their fight, the one who had given them all hope. If he didn't act, if he didn't find a way to save her, it would all be for nothing.

But the question that gnawed at him was simple: How?

He could feel the weight of the decision pressing down on him. Going to Kate might put the whole rebellion at risk. But going alone? That was suicide. Yet, the thought of leaving her there, suffering in silence, was worse than any fear he had ever felt. His mind kept returning to the last time he had seen her—the fire in her eyes as she had stood against Dev's forces, unflinching, even as they captured her.

She had saved so many, inspired so many, and Vihan had done nothing but search, search without ever finding her. Until now.

He closed his eyes, leaning against the cold wall of the alleyway, trying to steady himself. His emotions swirled, raw and unrelenting—fear, guilt, hope. The memories of their shared past only made it harder. He could still see her, standing before the crowd of villagers, her voice strong and clear as she called for them to fight back. That was the Adira he knew—the one who had never backed down, the one who had alwayss stood for what was right.

And now, she was lost in the dark, alone.

"I'll save you," he whispered to himself, his voice breaking. "I swear, I'll save you."

Tears stung his eyes, but he blinked them away. There was no time for weakness. No time for doubt. He would have to act, and soon. He just needed a plan. He would find a way, even if it meant going alone. Even if it meant risking everything.

For Adira, he would do anything.

The night stretched on, the weight of his decision pressing heavier on his chest. Vihan knew that whatever he did next, it would change everything. He had already come this far for her, and now, as he stood at the precipice, he could feel the enormity of the moment sinking in. He couldn't let fear stop him. Not now.

In the silence of the alleyway, as the stars flickered above, Vihan's mind cleared. There was no turning back.

For Adira. For everything they had once believed in.

He would save her. Even if it cost him everything.

The night was thick with tension as the campfire crackled in the center of the group. The flames danced wildly, casting long shadows on the faces of the rebels gathered around. Vihan stood at the edge, wiping away the last trace of his tears, his gaze locked on the fire. He felt the weight of everything Kate was about to share—the truth he hadn't spoken, the mission that would soon define their fate.

Kate stepped forward, his voice cutting through the murmurs of the crowd. There was an intensity in his eyes, a focus that sent a ripple of silence through the camp.

"I have news," Kate began, his voice steady, but fierce. "We've spent years fighting, bleeding, and losing people in our struggle against Dev. Many of you have given more than anyone should ever be asked to give. But tonight, we are on the verge of something greater. Something that will change everything."

The group leaned In, the crackling of the fire the only sound as they hung on his every word.

"We've found her," Kate said, pausing to let the words sink in. "The one who started this fire in all of us. The one who, even as a child, dared to defy the Chancellor. The one who made us believe we could fight back."

A murmur spread through the group. Faces lit with recognition, whispers of disbelief passing between them. They all knew who Kate was speaking about—her.

Adira.

Kate's eyes swept across the group, and he could see the realization dawning on them, the weight of what this meant. "After years of searching, we've found Adira."

The air around the campfire seemed to shift, the gravity of his words pulling everyone closer.

"She's alive," Kate continued, his voice filled with both pride and sorrow. "But she's in one of Dev's torture chambers. She's been there for years, leading warriors from within those hellish walls, fighting even when the world turned its back on her. She turned prisoners into soldiers, sparking courage in places filled with despair. And now, a riot is brewing inside. Her people are ready to fight back."

The murmurs grew louder, fear and anticipation battling for dominance in the hearts of the rebels. Kate held up his hand, silencing them once more.

"She's weak," he admitted, his voice lowering. "She's been through hell. But let me remind you—a warrior is always a warrior. And Adira... she is more than just a fighter. She's the fire that lit this rebellion. If we save her, we don't just gain a soldier back. We gain the leader we've needed all along. We gain hope."

Vihan's heart raced. He could barely breathe, knowing how close they were to rescuing her, to finally bringing her back. But doubt lingered in the eyes of some of the rebels, the uncertainty they had grown too familiar with.

One man stood up, his voice cutting through the silence. "Are we really risking everything for one person? A single woman? We've all fought. We've all bled for this. Do we put the whole rebellion at risk for this?"

A murmur of agreement rose from a few others, but Kate didn't flinch. He stepped forward, his voice like thunder.

"You question whether we risk it all for her?" Kate's voice sliced through the tense atmosphere, her eyes ablaze with fury as she stepped forward. "You don't know her. You don't know what she's done. This isn't just about one person—this is about the movement she built. Adira is one of the reason you're all standing here today. She sparked the fire that burns in each of us. She made us believe that Dev's regime could be brought to its knees.."

Kate paused, her gaze sweeping across the room, meeting the eyes of her comrades. "But listen—this isn't just about Adira. This is about every prisoner still trapped in Dev's hell—those who have suffered in silence for years, their voices crushed under his boot. These people are not just nameless victims; they are mothers, fathers, brothers, sisters—individuals with lives, dreams, and hopes that

Dev has shattered. We're fighting for their freedom too. They deserve our fight just as much as Adira does."

he took a deep breath, letting his words sink in. "Each one of those prisoners carries a story of loss and resilience. They are the forgotten, the oppressed, and the brutalized—people who have endured more than we can imagine. If we leave them behind, we lose more than just potential allies in battle; we lose our very humanity. We can't turn our backs on those who have suffered for so long."

His voice grew stronger, fueled by conviction. "We need them. They have strength we can't even see yet—strength born from suffering, anger, and an unyielding desire for justice. With them, we can forge a united front that Dev can't ignore. Together, we can break his hold on this land. Each rescued soul will not only bolster our numbers but also remind us of why we fight."

Kate's eyes burned with determination as he continued, "This mission is about more than Adira—it's about igniting a revolution for all those who've been silenced. When we free her, we'll also free them. And when that happens, we won't just have an army; we will have a movement—a tide of anger and hope crashing against Dev's walls. And with that tide, we'll finally have the power to reclaim our future."

The camp fell silent. Even those who had doubted felt the weight of his words. Vihan saw the flicker of recognition in their eyes, the moment when they began to understand who Adira truly was.

"And make no mistake," Kate continued, his voice lowering to a deadly calm, "this is not just about saving her. The people inside that prison are planning a riot. If we act now, we can turn that riot into a full-blown revolution. We can take down Dev's most feared stronghold. If we succeed, it will be the greatest victory we've ever had."

The fire roared higher, as if in response to Kate's words, the flames licking at the night sky.

Vihan's heart pounded. This was it. The moment they had been waiting for. But Kate wasn't done.

"You all doubt her because you don't know her story," Kate said, his eyes burning with intensity. "She may be weak now, but I've seen the fire that still burns in her. After everything she's been through, Adira remains unbroken. And when we bring her back, she will rise again. She will lead us, just as she always has."

The silence that followed was thick with tension. Vihan could feel the weight of the decision hanging in the air, the doubt lingering in the minds of those who still questioned the risk. But there was something else too—hope.

Finally, one of the doubters, a grizzled man who had seen more battles than most, stood up. His eyes locked on Kate, and then shifted to Vihan. "You're telling us she's the one who started it all? That she's the one who made you all believe?"

Vihan nodded, swallowing the lump in his throat. "She's more than just a fighter," he said, his voice filled with conviction. "She's one of the reason we're all still here."

The man hesitated for a moment, then slowly nodded, stepping back into the group. "Then we save her."

One by one, others echoed his words, their voices growing louder, more resolute. "We save her."

Kate's gaze flicked toward Vihan, and for a brief moment, their eyes met. Vihan nodded, a silent agreement passing between them.

CHAPTER 6
The Rescue...

The spy who had risked everything to pass the information about Adira to Kate had done more than just confirm her location—he had also handed over the blueprint of the torture chamber prison. A crumpled piece of paper, stained with sweat and grime, now held the key to their operation.

In the dimly lit hideout, Kate unfolded the blueprint, its inked lines and markings barely visible in the flickering torchlight. "This is it," he said, excitement and urgency mingling in his voice. "It shows the layout—the weak points in the prison. We can use the ventilation shafts and the unguarded corridors to our advantage. If we time our movements correctly, we'll be inside before anyone knows we've broken through."

Vihan's heart raced as he leaned closer, examining the path leading to Adira's cell. "We have to plan this carefully," he urged. "Every step must be precise. The riot will serve as our cover; while the guards are occupied with the chaos inside, we slip through the service tunnels and avoid their patrols. We'll reach Adira and the others before they can react."

Kate nodded, his mind racing with possibilities. "We'll need to strike swiftly. Once the riot escalates, the guards will be scattered, but we still need to be cautious. If we can create a diversion with our weapons—some well-placed fires or even a skirmish near the front entrance—it'll draw their attention away from us."

Vihan's gaze hardened, his resolve strengthening. "This isn't just about freeing Adira anymore. With this blueprint, we can liberate every prisoner suffering under

Dev's regime. We can't leave anyone behind. They've all endured too much."

Kate clenched his fists, determination blazing in his eyes. "Adira is our spark, but those prisoners—broken yet still fighting—they are the fuel. Together, they will ignite the fire that will consume Dev's empire."

As they finalized the plan, Kate gathered the team, spreading the blueprint before them. "Listen closely," he commanded, his voice steady. "We have our window. We'll set a diversion at the main entrance to draw the guards out. A few well-aimed shots and a fire near the gate will create enough chaos. While they're preoccupied, we'll slip through the service corridor."

The team nodded in understanding, their expressions a mix of fear and resolve. Vihan pointed to the blueprint. "Once we're inside, we'll head straight for the cell block. We can take out any guards in our path, but we must remain quiet. The last thing we want is an alarm sounded."

Kate scanned the faces of his comrades. "And remember," he added, locking eyes with each of them, "this mission is not just about saving Adira. We're also rescuing every single person trapped in that hellhole. Each one has endured suffering, and we must bring them back. We fight for their freedom, too."

The atmosphere crackled with determination as they prepared to move into position. They were not just rebels; they were liberators, ready to reclaim the light that had been stolen from them.

With adrenaline surging through their veins, they donned their armor and checked their weapons— guns loaded. The storm of rebellion was about to break, and the blueprint—their guide—was in their hands.

As they made their final preparations, Kate voice hardened. "Freedom is never voluntarily given by the oppressor; it must be demanded by the oppressed. Tonight, we demand it!"

With that rallying cry echoing in their hearts, they slipped into the shadows, ready to turn their plans into action, prepared to face whatever awaited them in the darkened corridors of the prison.

"Stay focused," Kate whispered to his team, urgency lacing his voice. "We've only got one shot at this."

The air was thick with tension as the rebels crouched in the shadows outside the prison, hearts racing in sync with the distant roars of chaos. Vihan's fingers tightened around his rifle, the cold metal grounding him. Adira was still weak from years of torture, but her spirit had become a beacon of defiance. She was their symbol of hope, and the riot inside was their only chance to break her out and liberate the other prisoners suffering under Dev's cruel regime.

Kate studied the crumpled blueprint of the prison in the dim light, his brow furrowed. "Listen up," he said, voice low but steady. "The riot inside is our cover. While the guards scramble to control the chaos, we'll slip through the service tunnels and cut them off at the main control room. If we can disable the gates and communications, we'll create a clear path for everyone."

Vihan nodded, adrenaline surging through him. "Once we breach the inner corridors, we need to move fast. Every moment we waste could cost lives. We find Adira and the others, and we get out—no exceptions."

"Right," Kate replied, his gaze sharp, eyes darting between the shadows. "Adira's the spark, but the other prisoners are the fuel. We can't leave anyone behind. They've all endured hell in here, and together, we can start a fire that Dev won't be able to extinguish."

The distant sounds of chaos grew louder, a cacophony of shouts and clashing into a primal symphony of rebellion. With a shared determination, they moved into position, nerves tingling with anticipation.

"Now!" Kate commanded, and they dashed toward the narrow opening of the service tunnel. The air was thick and dank, but the sound of rebellion propelled them forward.

As they raced through the darkened passage, Vihan's thoughts flickered to Adira. He could picture her in that cell—fragile yet fierce, still a warrior at heart. **They had to reach her, and they had to do it quickly.**

Emerging into a cramped corridor, Vihan and the rebels found themselves in the belly of the beast. The flickering torches cast eerie shadows, illuminating their anxious faces. Distant sounds of the riot echoed ominously, a reminder of the danger that loomed just beyond their reach.

"**This way,**" Kate urged, urgency creeping into his tone as he led them toward the cell block.

As they approached, the oppressive air thickened, each step heavy with dread. They could hear the guards shouting, barking orders as the riot spiraled out of control. Vihan's heart raced; **they had to act now.**

"**On my signal,**" Kate instructed, scanning the area. "When I say go, we charge in. Stick to the plan—get to the control room, disable the gates, and get Adira."

The anticipation in the air was electric. They crouched, adrenaline pumping through their veins as they listened. The tension was palpable, each second stretching into eternity.

"**Go!**" Kate shouted, and they surged forward, weapons drawn, adrenaline coursing through them like wildfire.

Chaos erupted as they burst into the main cell area rifles raised. Guards, caught off guard by the sudden intrusion, scrambled to respond. Vihan fired a shot, the bullet ringing true as it struck one of the guards. The others fell in line, unleashing a barrage of weapons against their foes. The gunfire echoed through the stone walls, each report drowning out the screams of the rioting prisoners.

But just as they gained ground, Just as they were making progress, a loud metal clang came from behind them. Vihan quickly turned around, his eyes widening in shock, as a group of guards rushed into the courtyard. The reinforcements had been called because of the chaos.

"**Fall back!**" Kate shouted, firing back, his voice strained. "We're outnumbered!"

Panic surged through Vihan as he glanced at the narrow hallway leading to the exit, blocked now by an impenetrable wall of guards. **Every instinct screamed for him to flee, but they couldn't abandon Adira.**

"**We need a distraction!**" he yelled, a plan forming in his mind. "Someone create a diversion—we can't get to the control room with them pressing in!"

Kate nodded, understanding flashing in his eyes. "I'll cover you! Get to the left flank!"

"**On it!**" Vihan replied, determination fueling his resolve. He sprinted toward a nearby storage area, grabbing a handful of explosives they had smuggled in the same prison.

"**Here goes nothing!**" he shouted, tossing the explosives toward the reinforcements. With a thunderous blast, debris rained down, creating a momentary gap as the guards scrambled to regain their composure.

"**Now!**" Kate bellowed, charging forward into the fray.

Vihan darted back to the group, heart pounding as they moved to capitalize on the confusion. They weaved through the chaos, darting between cells and makeshift barricades, every breath heavy with fear.

"**Adira!**" he called, desperation clawing at him. "Where are you?"

"**In here!**" a voice croaked from a nearby cell, weak but unmistakable. Vihan raced toward the sound, adrenaline driving him onward.

As he reached the cell, he fumbled with the lock, panic rising. "Hang on, Adira! I'm almost there!"

And then he saw her.

Amid the chaos, Adira emerged from the prison's interior, her face gaunt, her body bruised, but her spirit unbroken. She was weaker than the warrior he remembered, but the fire in her eyes burned brighter than ever. She gripped a stolen rifle with trembling hands, her breaths shallow, yet fierce determination was etched into every inch of her expression.

For a moment, the sight of her hit Vihan like a sledgehammer. She was the flame that had sparked this revolution, the force behind their fight, and now, in the heart of chaos, she was still leading.

Adira raised her weapon, her voice hoarse but commanding. "We fight! No more chains! No more suffering! For freedom!"

Her words cut through the noise like a blade, and those around her seemed to draw strength from her voice. The prisoners, many of whom had been broken by years of torture, now stood taller, inspired by her defiance. Even in her weakened state, Adira was still a warrior, a leader, and the hope they had all needed.

Vihan's heart swelled with pride as he saw her rally the prisoners. She had created soldiers out of the broken, turning fear into fire, just as she had done years before. And now, she was doing it again, right before his eyes.

But there was no time for admiration. The guards regrouped, pushing back hard with brutal force. Gunfire filled the air, and bodies fell around them. Vihan ducked behind cover, firing off shots as the rebels pushed forward, desperately trying to reach Adira's side.

Kate's voice boomed through the chaos. "Take their weapons! Turn them against them!"

The rebels surged forward, disarming the guards in close combat, turning stolen rifles and pistols on their enemies. The air was thick with smoke and blood, and the sounds of battle drowned out everything but the instinct to survive.

Adira, though weak, fought like a lioness. She moved with the precision of a seasoned warrior, her body remembering the motions even as her strength faltered. Each shot she fired was true, each command she gave inspiring those around her to fight harder.

Vihan saw it—the moment the tide began to turn. The prisoners, once overwhelmed by fear, now fought with the desperation of the truly free. They had nothing to lose but their chains, and with Adira leading the charge, they were unstoppable.

But it wasn't without cost. All around them, men and women fell, cut down by the relentless gunfire of Dev's soldiers. Vihan felt a bullet graze his arm, the sharp sting pulling him back into the moment. He ducked behind cover, his mind racing.

"Adira!" he shouted over the noise, his voice barely cutting through the chaos. "We need to move!"

But Adira wasn't listening. She was locked in a fight with a guard twice her size, their weapons discarded as they grappled in brutal hand-to-hand combat. She was clearly outmatched, her body weakened from years of torture, but her spirit remained fierce.

With a roar, she drove a knee into the guard's stomach, knocking the wind out of him before grabbing his dropped pistol and firing a shot into his chest. The guard crumpled, and Adira staggered, barely staying on her feet.

Vihan rushed to her side, his heart in his throat. "Adira, you need to rest. You're too weak—"

"I'm not done yet," she growled, wiping blood from her mouth. "We end this here."

Before Vihan could argue, a massive explosion rocked

As the dust settled from the battle, the rebel group, led by Adira, made their way back to the camp. The victory was hard-won, but the taste of it was bittersweet. The prison lay in ruins, the enemy camp obliterated, and the weapons and supplies they had seized were far beyond what they could have ever hoped for. Tanks, armories, guns—everything they needed to fuel the next phase of the rebellion. They had accomplished the impossible, but the toll was heavy. Adira had fought fiercely, but the years of torture had taken their toll, and she collapsed as soon as they reached the safety of the camp.

Vihan stood by her side the entire time, his heart heavy as she lay unconscious for days, her body battling to regain its strength. The camp bustled around them, people coming and going, but every set of eyes seemed to linger on Adira—the woman they had once doubted, now their greatest hope. The people whispered of her courage, her fire, her unyielding spirit. The story of her fight in the prison had already spread through the camp, and even those who had questioned the risk of saving her now watched her with awe and respect.

When she finally regained consciousness, Adira was different. There was a quiet intensity in her eyes, a deep resolve. She didn't waste time—once she was strong enough to stand, she threw herself into training, determined to regain every ounce of strength she had lost. Vihan and the others trained alongside her, helping her relearn the skills that had once made her a warrior. But it didn't take long before it became clear that Adira was far more than just another fighter. She was a force of nature.

Her recovery was nothing short of remarkable. In mere days, she had mastered the weapons they had taken from the prison—the guns, the knives, even the heavier artillery. She moved with a fierce precision that left the others in awe, her mind sharp as ever, strategizing with Kate and the rest of the leadership. Even in the heat of practice, her focus never wavered, and those who had once doubted her found themselves watching her every move, captivated by the fire she carried within.

Vihan couldn't take his eyes off her. Every day, he saw her growing stronger, reclaiming the fierce warrior she had once been. She practiced relentlessly, often late into the night, pushing her body to the limit, her determination burning like a beacon in the darkness. Vihan knew she was still weak in some ways—her body hadn't fully recovered—but none of that seemed to matter to Adira. She fought with a relentless drive, as if the pain and exhaustion only fueled her further.

In the evenings, after the day's training, the camp would gather, sharing quiet conversations by the fire. It was during these moments that Vihan noticed something remarkable. The same people who had once hesitated, who had questioned Kate's decision to save her, now watched Adira with newfound respect. They no longer saw her as just another rebel. They saw her as something more—as the warrior she had always been, the leader they needed.

Kate himself had been watching her closely, a quiet smile tugging at the corners of his mouth whenever he saw her in action. One night, after a particularly grueling training session, Kate stood beside Vihan, both of them watching as Adira led a group of rebels in combat drills. Her movements were swift, calculated, commanding. She had taken control without ever needing to raise her voice.

"She's going to do something great," Kate said softly, his voice filled with a quiet admiration.

Vihan nodded, his heart swelling with pride. "She already has."

Kate chuckled, his eyes never leaving Adira. "No, this is just the beginning. There's a storm coming, Vihan. And she's going to be at the center of it."

CHAPTER 7
The Pain...

Around the fire, the soft crackling of wood provided the only warmth in the dark night. The camp was filled with tired soldiers, their faces etched with both pain and determination. Tonight was different though, as Adira stood at the center, her presence commanding every eye. For days, the camp had been buzzing with questions—about the torture chamber, about the suffering she endured. Vihan stood on the edge of the circle, his heart racing, knowing that tonight would reveal more than just her story.

Adira cleared her throat, her voice firm yet haunted by memories of unimaginable pain. "I wasn't always this strong," she began. "In that chamber, they broke us, bit by bit. I was beaten from the very first day, whipped, starved, mocked—all to make me break. But I didn't. Even when Minervan came... I didn't."

The crowd shifted, confused whispers among them. "Minervan?" someone asked.

Adira's eyes darkened. "Yes. Minervan, the man my father trusted. The man who was supposed to be our ally. One night, he came to the prison. I was beaten badly, barely conscious, but I saw him. He laughed as he looked at me, a cruel, greedy smile that still haunts me."

Vihan clenched his fists, his hatred for Minervan bubbling inside him. He remembered the betrayal, the news of Minervan's rise to power under Dev's regime

As Minervan's words echoed in the chamber, I felt the heat of fury ignite within me, burning away the pain. My body was weak from days of beatings and torture, yet my spirit remained untamed. This man, once trusted by my father, now stood before me as the very embodiment of betrayal. His smug smile twisted grotesquely in the flickering light of my cell, and I could feel the darkness emanating from him like a thick fog.

"You don't understand power, Adira," he sneered, pacing around my bound figure, his voice dripping with contempt. "Your father was a fool. He could have had everything, but he chose to fight Dev. And for what? For people who don't even care about themselves? People who lack the strength to stand up. But now? They follow me. I lead, they listen. You're just a girl who has no idea what real power is."

My heart thundered in my chest, and I fought against my chains, every fiber of my being screaming to resist him. "You're a coward, Minervan," I spat, tasting the metallic tang of blood in my mouth. "A traitor who killed his own friend for a piece of Dev's table scraps. That's not power. That's desperation."

His expression shifted in an instant, the smug grin fading into a cold, violent anger. "You insolent girl!" he roared, storming toward me. I braced myself as he backhanded me across the face. Pain exploded, my head snapping to the side, but I refused to let a sound escape my lips.

"You think you can talk to me like that?!" he bellowed, striking me again, harder this time. My body slumped against the chains, rattling as I struggled to hold onto consciousness. He grabbed my hair, yanking my head back, and I could feel his hot breath against my cheek. "I own this town! I own these people! And you—" He slammed me against the wall, the chains cutting into my skin. "—you are nothing!"

But I wouldn't let him break me. Even as pain coursed through my body, I met his gaze with unbroken defiance. I refused to show fear, refused to let him see the flicker of doubt he so desperately sought. I was not the girl he thought I was; I was more than my injuries, more than his twisted desires.

"I am not afraid of you," I said, my voice steady despite the tremors within. "You may have the chains, but I have the will to fight. You may think you own this town, but the heart of its people beats with courage. You can't crush that."

Minervan's face contorted with rage, but I saw the flicker of uncertainty in his eyes. In that moment, I realized my power. He might have the upper hand, but

I had something he could never possess—hope, resilience, and the fire of rebellion burning deep within me.

Minervan drew back, his rage barely contained, the malice in his eyes igniting a familiar fire within me. He began to pace, ranting with fervor. "You really think you can make a difference? A single girl, standing against the might of Dev's army? I'll show you what happens to those who defy me."

I braced myself as he pulled a baton from his belt, the cruel intent behind his swing sending a chill down my spine. Instinct kicked in just in time; I twisted away painfully against the restraints. The baton slammed into the wall beside me, sparks flying, and I couldn't help but feel a surge of adrenaline coursing through my veins.

"Fight all you want," he snarled, his voice dripping with contempt. "But you'll break. Everyone breaks."

His words echoed in my mind, but I could feel the weight of my chains begin to loosen as I caught sight of a broken rod beneath the debris in the corner of the cell. A flicker of hope ignited within me, and I formulated a desperate plan. As Minervan approached, baton raised for another blow, I jerked my chains violently, feeling them yield slightly.

With a primal roar, he swung again, but I yanked my chained arm free with all my strength, ducking just in time. The baton whooshed past me, and I seized the moment. My chained wrist became a weapon as I slammed it into Minervan's jaw with a sickening crack. The sound echoed, a sweet symphony of defiance.

He stumbled backward, shock and fury dancing in his eyes, but there was no time to waste. I lunged for the jagged metal rod, wrapping my fingers around it just as he regained his footing. As he charged, I twisted my body, bringing the rod up and driving it into his stomach.

Minervan gasped, his eyes widening in disbelief as blood spilled from the wound. I felt an overwhelming surge of fury rise within me. This was for my father, for every moment I had been trapped in despair. With a fierce scream, I pulled the rod free and thrust it into him again, hitting him square in the chest.

His breath came in ragged gasps, eyes pleading. "You... you..." he stammered, blood pouring from his mouth, shock dawning on his face.

"Enough," I said coldly, my heart racing as I stood over him, my face smeared with blood and fury. "This is for my father." I delivered the final blow, driving the rod into his throat with a swift, brutal motion.

Minervan's body hit the floor with a heavy thud, life draining from his eyes as he gurgled his last breath. I collapsed to my knees, panting, every ounce of strength draining from me. I had done it—Minervan, the traitor, was dead.

But my victory was short-lived. The guards outside had heard the commotion and stormed into the cell, their eyes wide with shock at the sight of Minervan's lifeless body on the floor.

Without hesitation, they lunged at me. I barely had time to rise before the first soldier swung at me. I dodged, using my chains to deflect the blow, but the second guard grabbed me from behind, locking my arms.

I struggled, twisting and kicking, but the guards were strong, and my body was weak from the torture. The third guard aimed a punch at my ribs, pain exploding through me, but I wouldn't give up. Not now.

With a surge of adrenaline, I swung my head back, smashing it into the nose of the guard holding me. He cried out in pain, loosening his grip just enough for me to slip free. I grabbed the rod from the floor and swung it at the nearest soldier, catching him in the side of the head. He crumpled to the ground, and the other two guards hesitated, stunned by my ferocity.

I fought like a woman possessed. I blocked their attacks, using my chains as both shield and weapon, swinging them with deadly precision. Blow after blow, I felt my strength waning, but I pressed on.

After what felt like an eternity, the last guard fell, and I stood amidst the carnage, my body battered and broken, but my spirit unbowed. I had survived the impossible. I had killed the traitor.

But even in this moment of triumph, I knew it was just the beginning. I collapsed to the floor, the pain of my injuries catching up to me. Distant clatter of boots approached—reinforcements. I wouldn't be able to fight them all, not like this.

Yet, I had done more than anyone thought possible. I had killed Minervan. Even if they captured me again, I knew that fire would spread. I had given the people hope, and that flame would burn bright, no matter what Dev or his men tried to extinguish it.

With the last of my strength, I raised my head, defiant in the face of overwhelming odds, ready to fight for what was right.

With her final burst of strength, Adira raised her head, defiant even in the face of overwhelming odds.

Tears welled up in the eyes of many around the fire. They hadn't known the depths of her suffering, and now, seeing her still standing strong, they felt a spark—something more than fear, something like hope.

Vihan's heart shattered as he watched her. He had known her since childhood, had waited for the right moment to reveal who he truly was to her. But now, standing there, seeing her strength, he felt unworthy. How could he possibly console her?

As the crowd dispersed, leaving Adira alone by the fire, Vihan slowly approached her. His voice was low, filled with the weight of his own guilt. "Adira... you've been through more than anyone could bear."

She turned, her eyes fierce, but there was a softness in them for the first time in days. "Vihan," she said, her voice quiet. "How long are you going to pretend you're not the boy I knew from our village?"

Vihan froze, his breath catching in his throat.

"How long, Vihan?" she repeated, stepping closer to him. "How long are you going to hide from me? I know you've been waiting. You're the Vihan who used to follow me around, always watching out for me, always waiting for me. You're my

Vihan."

Vihan's eyes met hers, filled with both fear and longing. He had spent years waiting for this moment, for her to recognize him, but now that she had, he didn't know how to respond. "Adira, I—" he began, his voice trembling.

She shook her head, placing a hand on his chest. "You've always been there, even when I didn't know it. But now, I see you. I see everything."

Vihan closed his eyes, the pain of his own losses flooding back to him. His family was gone, the town he loved destroyed, and yet here she was, standing before him—strong, fierce, and alive. For the first time in years, he felt something other than rage. He felt hope.

Together, they stood by the fire, their pasts intertwined, and for the first time in a long while, they both believed that maybe, just maybe, they could find a way to bring down Dev's reign of terror, once and for all.

As the days passed, Adira's presence in the camp grew larger than life. She wasn't just training to become a warrior again—she was igniting a fire within the people. The camp felt different now, more united, more driven. The rebels, once fractured and doubtful, now trained with a renewed sense of purpose, their eyes filled with the same fire that burned in Adira's. Even those who had questioned saving her now spoke of her with reverence, their doubts long gone.

Adira had become more than just a symbol. She was the heart of the rebellion.

One evening, as the camp gathered around the fire, Adira stood before them, her eyes burning with intensity. She spoke of the battles ahead, of the fight they would have to take to Dev, and of the people they had lost along the way. Her voice was steady, strong, and the silence around her was heavy with anticipation.

"We've come this far because we've fought together," she said, her voice carrying over the crowd. "We've bled, we've lost, but we've never broken. And we won't break now."

The rebels listened, their eyes locked on her. Vihan stood at the back of the crowd, his heart swelling with pride. This was the Adira he had always known—the fierce, unyielding leader who had once inspired him to fight.

"We have everything we need," she continued, her voice fierce. "Weapons. Armor. Strength. But most of all, we have each other. And as long as we stand together, we will win."

The crowd erupted in cheers, the sound of their voices echoing through the camp, filling the night with hope and determination. Vihan felt a tear slip down his cheek as he watched Adira stand before them, her chin raised, her eyes blazing with purpose.

This was just the beginning. The war against Dev was far from over, but with Adira at their side, Vihan knew they could face whatever came next. She was their leader, their warrior, their hope.

And she was unstoppable.

CHAPTER 8

Crushing Hope: The Fall of Adira

Dev sat on his towering throne, fists clenched in pure rage. His cold, calculating eyes scanned the room, where his advisors trembled under the weight of his silence. The air was thick with tension, every breath held in anticipation of his next words. His jaw tightened as the news was whispered into his ear—Adira had escaped. The very woman who had already proven herself as a spark of rebellion had slipped through his iron grip.

He slammed his fist onto the armrest, the crack of wood splintering echoed through the chamber. "How is this possible?!" he bellowed, his voice reverberating with a chilling fury. "I had her in chains, beaten, broken. And now she's out there—somewhere—free!"

His generals exchanged fearful glances, no one daring to meet his eyes. Dev stood, his towering presence casting a long shadow across the room. His face was twisted with a mixture of disbelief and seething anger.

"If this gets out, if even a whisper of her survival reaches the people, everything we've built—everything I control—will unravel!" He paced back and forth like a caged animal, his mind racing. He knew what Adira represented. She was not just a woman; she was a symbol. A symbol of defiance. Of hope. And hope was something he could not allow to exist.

Turning sharply toward his top general, Dev's eyes blazed with murderous intent. "She must be found. I don't care how long it takes or what it costs. Deploy every soldier, every spy. Search every village, every corner of the land. I want her dragged before me—alive or dead. But if she's alive, I want her broken in front of everyone."

His voice dropped into a low, venomous growl. "This time, we kill her hope in front of the people. I want them to see what happens when they dare to defy me. They will know what awaits them if they ever think of rebellion again."

The general, sweating under the weight of Dev's fury, nodded quickly. "Yes, Chancellor. We'll expand the search immediately."

Dev strode toward the massive window overlooking his empire, his knuckles white as he gripped the railing. Below, his legions of soldiers marched in formation, a sea of red uniforms and steel. "And send in the spies. Double the numbers, triple them if needed. I want no stone unturned. I want her place of hiding found before the week is out."

He turned back to his men, his voice a deadly whisper. "When we find her, we will not just capture her. We will make an example of her. I will strip her of every last shred of dignity, and when the people watch her die, they will know—there is no hope. Only fear. I am their master, and they will obey."

The tension in the room was suffocating as Dev's cold, calculated rage permeated every corner. His face, now calm, betrayed nothing but lethal intent.

"No one will save her," he muttered to himself, his fingers drumming against the window ledge. "No one escapes me. Not her. Not anyone."

As his spies and soldiers were sent out like wolves hunting their prey, Dev's mind was already crafting the scene. He would not just kill her; he would crush her before the very eyes of the people. The hope that she had ignited would be doused in blood, and the rebellion, however small, would die with her.

"Adira," he whispered darkly, "you will not be a hero. You will be a reminder of the price of defiance."

With that, Dev retreated into his chambers, his mind already plotting his next moves.

CHAPTER 9
A Hero's Sacrifice

The night was heavy with the stench of burning wood and fear as Kate Nilan, leader of the rebel group, stood before his people in the hidden camp. His presence was commanding, his figure strong despite the weariness etched into his face. Around him, the young fighters—those who had chosen to stand against Chancellor Dev—waited in silence, their eyes locked on him, the man who had given them a purpose.

Kate had always been their shield, gathering them, guiding them, and fighting for those who could no longer fight for themselves. His heart had long been hardened by the weight of the atrocities Dev had committed. But tonight, it was different. Tonight, the fire burning inside him was deeper—angrier.

He looked around the circle, his eyes settling on each face, and his voice, though quiet, carried the weight of a storm. "I've received word from our Intel," he began, his tone dark, "the people in the nearby village… they're not just suffering. They're being enslaved. Forced to work in Dev's refineries and mines like animals. Anyone who resists is taken to the torture chambers. Many of them are dying, and those who survive… they're broken."

A murmur of disbelief spread through the group, shock mixing with anger. They had heard rumors of Dev's cruelty, of his grip tightening on the lands beyond their hidden sanctuary, but hearing it confirmed sent chills through their bones.

One of the younger rebels, a boy barely in his twenties, clenched his fists. "We've saved people from his prisons, we've fought his soldiers, but this… this is something else. What do we do, Kate?"

Kate's jaw tightened, the firelight flickering across the deep lines of his face. His mind raced, the responsibility of these lives heavy on his shoulders. "We act," he said, his voice firm. "We cannot stand by and let Dev take more innocent lives. If we don't help them, if we don't strike now, those people will be worked to death."

Adira, who stood at Kate's side, her face pale with the weight of the news, took a step forward. "How many are we talking about? How many people are enslaved?"

Kate glanced at her, his eyes filled with sorrow. "'It's devastating. Hundreds, maybe even thousands, are suffering. Dev is treating them like disposable commodities, exploiting the mines and refineries for his own gain. To him, their lives are just resources to be used for profit."

He paused, anguish etching deeper lines on his face. "These people are forced to work long hours, toiling under brutal conditions, all while barely receiving enough food to survive. Their suffering fuels his ambition, and he cares nothing for their pain."

The group was silent for a long moment, the fire crackling softly as the weight of Kate's words sank in. These weren't just strangers—these were their people, families, and friends from the nearby villages. Their fight had always been about survival, but now it was about something more. Now, it was about justice.

Vihan stepped forward, his voice thick with emotion. "If we're going to do this, we need a plan. Dev's men are everywhere, and those refineries are heavily guarded. This isn't like freeing prisoners from the torture chambers; This..this will require everything we have."

Kate nodded, his expression hardening. "I know. But we've faced worse odds before. We've survived, and we've fought back. We will do it again. These people are counting on us."

He paused, his gaze sweeping across the group. "This isn't just a fight for survival anymore. This is about standing up for those who can't fight for themselves. This is about making sure that Dev knows we will not bow, we will not break, and we will never let him destroy us."

The group nodded In solemn agreement. They were young, some barely out of childhood, but their eyes burned with the fire of rebellion, of defiance. They had chosen this path knowing the risks, and now, with Kate leading them, they would walk it until the end.

Kate looked at them, pride swelling in his chest despite the danger that lay ahead. "Prepare yourselves. Tomorrow, we go to the village. We save those people. And we show Dev that his tyranny has met its match."

The firelight flickered, casting long shadows across the determined faces of the rebels. Tomorrow, they would face hell. But tonight, in this moment, they were more than a ragtag group of rebels. They were hope, they were resistance, and they were ready to fight.

As the group dispersed, Kate remained by the fire, his eyes distant, his mind already planning the coming battle. He knew the price of defiance. He knew what it meant to go against a force as ruthless as Dev. But he also knew this—if they didn't fight for those who couldn't, no one else would.

And he wasn't about to let that happen.

The night stretched on as Kate and his team huddled around a hastily drawn map of the refinery and mines. The fire at the center of their camp flickered with a dangerous energy, mirroring the resolve in their hearts. They were few, a ragtag group of rebels who had been pushed to their limits, but tonight, none of that mattered. They were prepared to fight an army.

Kate's face was set in stone as he began laying out the plan. "We don't have the numbers to face them head-on," he said, his voice steady but intense. "Hundreds of soldiers will be waiting for us. But we do have something they don't expect—surprise and strategy."

Adira stood by his side, her eyes scanning the faces of the rebels who were listening with fierce determination. In her hand, she clutched one of the weapons they had recovered—an automatic rifle taken during her escape from the torture chambers. That night, Kate and the team had risked their lives to save her, and now, they were preparing for another impossible mission.

Her voice was low but resolute. "We use what we have—these weapons, our knowledge of the terrain, and our will to fight. They might have numbers, but they don't have our fire."

Vihan stepped forward, his expression grim. "And what about the villagers? If we attack, Dev's men will use them as shields, or worse."

Kate nodded, knowing the risk. "That's why we need to strike strategically. We hit them fast and hard, create enough chaos to disrupt their defenses, and get the villagers out before they even realize what's happening. If we can take out the key points—the watchtowers and the weapon caches—they'll be scrambling to organize, and that's when we make our move."

He motioned to the map, his finger tracing a route through the dense forest surrounding the mines. "We'll split into two groups. One will take the south entrance, where the guards are fewer. The other group will attack from the north, hitting the watchtowers first. Once the towers are down, we'll move in on the refinery and free as many villagers as we can."

Adira's heart pounded in her chest as she absorbed the weight of their plan. It was bold, risky, and teetering on the edge of insanity. But it was their only chance. "And the soldiers?" she asked, her voice sharp with focus.

Kate met her gaze, unflinching. "We'll have to deal with them as they come. We're outnumbered, but they'll be caught off guard. That's our only advantage. If we can create enough confusion, we might just pull this off."

The fire crackled, filling the silence as the group exchanged glances. The tension was palpable, thick enough to choke on. Each of them knew what was at stake. This wasn't just about freeing the villagers—it was about striking a blow against Dev's empire, a blow that could turn the tide of their rebellion.

Jorik, one of their Intel contacts, spoke up from the shadows. "The weapons you recovered from the torture chamber will help, but it's not just firepower we need. We'll need to be smart, outthink them. We'll have only a few minutes before Dev's forces send reinforcements."

Adira's hand tightened around the grip of her rifle. "Then we make every minute count."

Vihan nodded, stepping closer. "If we fail, we die. But if we succeed… we cripple Dev's grip on this region. We give the people hope."

Kate's voice dropped lower, almost a whisper, but it carried a weight that settled in each of their hearts. "This is the fight we've been waiting for. We may not have numbers, but we have purpose. We have reason. And tonight, we fight for those who can't."

"His words lingered in the air, charged with emotion. For a moment, they all stood in silence, fully aware of the weight of what was ahead. The villagers they needed to save, the risks they would take—it was all tied together in this one bold act of defiance."

"We're ready," Adira said, breaking the silence, her voice strong and unyielding.

Kate nodded, his eyes shining with both pride and worry. "Then let's move."

The night of the attack came swiftly, a veil of darkness descending over the forest as the two groups split and crept toward the refinery. Adira's heart pounded in her ears as she led her small team through the dense undergrowth, their movements silent, their breaths held. Every step felt like a step closer to fate—either victory or death.

The refinery loomed ahead like a towering fortress of steel and fire, its smokestacks spewing thick, black smoke into the dark sky. The rhythmic clanking of machinery echoed through the still night, while the faint glow of torches outlined the guards patrolling the perimeter. The sight was daunting—a stark reminder of the immense challenge that lay before them.

But Adira pushed the fear down, keeping her focus on the mission. Behind her, Vihan and the others moved with practiced precision. They had trained for this moment, and now, all they had to do was execute.

From the north, a low thud echoed across the landscape—the watchtowers. Kate's team had struck first, disabling the towers just as planned. The guards on the south side turned in confusion, their attention diverted.

"Now," Adira whispered, motioning her team forward.

With lightning speed, they moved in, crossing the open ground toward the refinery's entrance. The guards were still distracted by the attack on the towers when Adira raised her rifle and fired. The shots rang out in the night, taking down two soldiers before they even had a chance to react.

Chaos erupted. Shouts filled the air as Dev's men scrambled to organize, rushing toward the watchtowers where they believed the main attack was happening. But they were too slow. By the time they realized the real threat was coming from the south, it was too late.

Adira's team surged forward, cutting through the soldiers like a knife. The weapons they had recovered from the torture chamber were crude but effective, and they used them to devastating effect. Vihan, his face a mask of grim determination, led the charge, taking down enemies with brutal efficiency.

Inside the refinery, panic spread as workers and soldiers alike tried to flee. Adira reached the central chamber, where the villagers were being held—thin, broken figures who looked more like ghosts than people. The sight nearly broke her heart, but she didn't have time to dwell on it.

"We're here to free you," she shouted, her voice cutting through the chaos. "Follow us, and we'll get you out!"

The villagers stared at her in disbelief, too stunned to move. But slowly, hope flickered in their eyes, and they began to follow. One by one, they emerged from the darkness, stumbling toward freedom.

Outside, the battle raged on, but the rebels were winning. Kate's strategy had worked—the confusion, the surprise attack, the precision. They had turned the tide.

As the last of the villagers stumbled out of the refinery, Adira looked back, scanning the chaotic battlefield. The sounds of gunfire and explosions filled the air, but amidst the noise, she caught sight of Kate on the far side of the refinery. He was standing at the edge of a collapsing structure, his eyes locked on a group of people—villagers who had been separated from the rest.

Adira's heart tightened as she watched him. "Kate!" she shouted over the noise. He turned to her, his face covered in dirt and blood, but his expression was calm, resolute.

"I found more survivors!" Kate called back, his voice hoarse but determined. He motioned to the small group—half a dozen people huddled together in fear, their faces gaunt and terrified. "Go, Adira! Lead the others! I'll get them out!"

Adira's pulse quickened, an icy fear gripping her chest. "No, we go together! We're almost out!"

Kate shook his head, a small, sad smile crossing his face. "You need to get them to safety. We don't have time, Adira. I'll handle this."

She knew what he meant, even before he said the words. The soldiers were closing in, the window for escape growing smaller by the second. If they waited any longer, none of them would make it out.

Adira's throat tightened. "Kate, don't. We'll find another way. We can still save them."

But Kate's expression remained steady, the weight of leadership—and sacrifice—settling on his shoulders. "This is what we fight for," he said softly, his voice carrying over the distance between them. "You lead them, Adira. You've always been stronger than you know. Now go."

Tears pricked at the corners of her eyes, but she couldn't let them fall. Not now. Not when she had to be strong. Adira clenched her fists, her voice barely above a whisper. "I'll come back for you."

Kate gave her one last nod. "I know."

Adira hesitated, her heart screaming at her to stay, to fight with him. But in that moment, she knew what Kate was doing. He wasn't just saving the last of the villagers—he was making sure the others had a chance to live, even if it meant he wouldn't.

With a sharp breath, Adira turned, calling to Vihan and the others. "Get them out of here! Now!"

The group of rebels, along with the rescued villagers, moved swiftly toward the forest, disappearing into the darkness as Adira led them. Every step felt like a betrayal, like she was leaving a part of herself behind. But Kate's voice echoed in her mind: This is what we fight for.

As they fled, the sounds of gunfire and screams continued to erupt behind them. Adira couldn't look back. She couldn't bear to see what was happening.

Back at the refinery, Kate stood with the small group of villagers, his heart heavy but resolute. The soldiers were closing in, their boots pounding the ground as they swept through the rubble. He knew his time was running out, but he wasn't afraid. Not anymore.

He turned to the villagers, their terrified faces reflecting the hopelessness of their situation. "Stay low," he whispered, his voice calm despite the chaos around him. "I'll protect you."

He raised his weapon, the last of the rifles they had scavenged from the torture chambers, and aimed it at the approaching soldiers. His hands were steady, his mind clear. He knew what had to be done.

As the first wave of soldiers rushed forward, Kate opened fire, each shot ringing out like a final defiance against Dev's tyranny. The soldiers fell, but more replaced them, swarming like a tidal wave of darkness. Kate fought with everything he had, but he was only one man against an army.

The villagers screamed as the soldiers closed in, and in a moment of sheer brutality, Kate was overrun. A blade pierced his side, followed by another, and then another. His body collapsed under the weight of the assault, but even as he fell, his eyes remained fierce, unyielding.

He had given everything for this fight, for these people, and he would die knowing he had done everything he could.

Far in the distance, Adira and the others reached the edge of the forest, the sounds of battle fading behind them. As they stopped to catch their breath, Adira's mind raced, her heart heavy with dread. She knew Kate wouldn't be following. Not this time.

Vihan approached her, his face pale with the weight of what had just happened. "Adira…" he started, but his words trailed off. He didn't need to say it. They both knew.

Adira's heart broke in that moment, her legs nearly giving out beneath her. But she couldn't afford to crumble, not now. Kate had made his choice, and she had to honor it. She had to lead them—just like he had asked.

With a deep breath, she steadied herself, wiping the tears from her eyes. "We'll come back for him," she whispered, more to herself than anyone else. "But first, we need to finish what he started."

The others nodded, though their faces were grim with loss.

As they moved deeper into the forest, Adira felt the weight of Kate's sacrifice settle into her soul. She would carry it with her, always. And one day, she would make sure Dev paid for everything he had done.

For Kate, for the villagers, and for everyone who had suffered under Dev's reign.

This was far from over.

CHAPTER 10
The Last Hope...

Adira stood by the flickering fire, her eyes tracing the embers as they floated into the dark sky. The whispers around the camp had grown louder in the last hour—everyone knew now. The truth had spread like the flames licking the wood in front of her. Chancellor Dev had killed Kate Nilan, their brave leader, in cold blood. Kate had been the only one daring enough to stand up for the enslaved workers in the Chancellor's mines and refineries, and it had cost him his life.

Adira's chest tightened. Kate's death had left a gaping void in the team, but more than grief, there was fear—and fury. She could see it in their eyes as they glanced at her, waiting for some kind of plan, a way to bring down the man who had shattered their trust. But how? Dev was as ruthless as he was powerful, and the team was on the edge of breaking, their morale dangerously low.

She pulled her coat tighter around her shoulders, the cool night air pressing down like a weight. Dev had to be stopped, not just for Kate, but for the countless others suffering under his thumb. But one wrong move and they'd all be as dead as Kate, lying in some unmarked grave in the wilderness.

Adira closed her eyes, replaying her last conversation with Kate before his fatal mission. He'd been so sure, so confident that they could make a difference. "People are more than their fear," he'd said. "Sometimes, they just need to be reminded of it."

A flicker of an Idea sparked in her mind. Dev thrived on control, on keeping people too afraid to fight back. But if she could remind them of what Kate had believed, ignite the flame of resistance in them, maybe—just maybe—they could turn the tide. They didn't need brute force. They needed unity. They needed hope.

Adira glanced over at the others, her gaze settling on the faces filled with anger and sorrow. It was time to turn that into resolve.

"We can't let Kate's death be in vain," she said softly, her voice cutting through the quiet murmurs. The group looked up at her, their expressions hard but uncertain.

She took a deep breath, the words coming easier now. "Dev thinks he's untouchable because he rules through fear. But we have something stronger. We have each other. We have the truth. And if we stand together, he can't break us."

A few heads nodded slowly, the firelight reflecting in their eyes.

"We'll take back what's ours. For Kate. For everyone he's crushed."

She knew it wouldn't be easy. Dev was cunning, ruthless, and he wouldn't hesitate to kill again if it meant keeping his grip on power. But for the first time since Kate's death, she felt a sense of purpose stir within her.

Tomorrow, they would start to fight back—not with weapons, but with the one thing Chancellor Dev could never control: hope.

The fire crackled softly, casting a warm glow over the tense faces gathered around it. Adira stood at the center, her eyes focused on the flames, as though searching them for the courage she needed. The group was silent, waiting for her to speak. Each one of them had lost something to Dev—friends, family, freedom. And now, with their leader Kate gone, they were looking to her. But how could she ask them to risk everything?

Vihan's voice cut through the silence, filled with frustration. "We need to defeat him, Adira. Whatever it takes. But we need more than just anger. We need a plan."

Adira nodded, her gaze still fixed on the fire. She could feel the weight of the moment, the pressure building inside her chest. She took a deep breath, her father's lessons echoing in her mind like whispers from the past.

"I've been thinking," she began quietly, but her voice grew stronger with each word. "You've all heard the rumors. About Arya's Wrath."

The name sent a ripple through the group. People stiffened, their eyes widening as the weight of those words settled over them. Vihan frowned, his voice laced with disbelief. "Arya's Wrath? That's… that's just a myth, isn't it?"

Adira turned to face them, her eyes burning with an intensity they hadn't seen before. "No, it's not a myth," she said, her voice clear and unwavering. "It's real. My father—before he died—he found out the truth. Arya's Wrath is Dev's greatest secret. A vault, hidden away, filled with his wealth—gold, money, weapons. Everything he's stolen from us, from everyone. If we can find it... if we can take it... we can strip him of everything. Without it, he's nothing."

The group murmured In disbelief, but there was a flicker of hope in their voices now, a faint light in the darkness.

Vihan leaned forward, his eyes narrowing. "And how do we know it's not just another story? Another rumor?"

Adira's gaze darkened as she took a step closer, her voice softer but filled with raw emotion. "I know because my father dedicated his life to finding it. He believed in it, and he was killed for it. Not just by Dev—but by someone he trusted. Someone Dev corrupted."

The firelight flickered across her face, but it couldn't mask the pain in her eyes. For a moment, the group was silent, stunned by the weight of her words. They knew about her father, knew he had been a brave man, but this… this was personal.

"A plan?" someone whispered from the back of the group.

Adira nodded, her voice steady now. "Yes. My father worked on a plan. He taught me everything he knew before he died. And I learned more over the years. Arya's Wrath isn't just some ordinary safe. It's massive. It's said to be able to hold over ten thousand tons of wealth and weapons. And it's the strongest, most secure vault ever created. But… it has a weakness. A way in."

Vihan's eyes narrowed, skepticism still etched on his face. "And how do you know all this?"

Adira swallowed hard, her voice growing softer. "Because when I was a child, my father would teach me these things. He'd tell me stories, make me memorize every detail of the vault. At the time, I didn't understand why. I just thought it was… another lesson. But now I know. He was preparing me for this. For the day we would have to take it back."

The group was silent, the air thick with emotion. Adira looked around at them, her voice trembling slightly but filled with determination. "I know you've all lost hope. We've lost so much—our friends, our families. Kate… he's gone because of Dev. But this… this is our chance. If we find Arya's Wrath, if we take everything Dev has, he'll have nothing left to hold over us. We'll be free."

A long silence followed, and for a moment, Adira feared she hadn't reached them. But then Vihan spoke, his voice quieter now, thoughtful. "And where is this vault?"

"That's the hard part," Adira admitted. "No one knows exactly where it is. My father believed it was hidden deep within the refinery, where Dev keeps his operations running. But we'll have to sneak in. We'll have to take a risk. But if we succeed, we can finally end this. We can stop Dev."

Vihan looked down for a moment, then back up at her, his expression softer than before. "You think you can get us inside?"

Adira nodded, her voice filled with quiet confidence. "Yes. I know I can."

The group exchanged glances, and then one by one, they nodded in agreement. Vihan took a step closer to her, his expression resolute. "Alright. I'm with you. We're with you. Whatever it takes."

Adira's heart swelled with emotion, a deep sense of purpose filling her chest. This was what her father had prepared her for. This was what Kate had died for. And now, together, they would finish it.

She looked around at them, her voice stronger than it had been all night. "We do this for Kate. We do this for everyone Dev has hurt. We find that vault, and we take back what's ours. And when we do, Dev won't just fall. He'll be erased."

The fire crackled louder, as though echoing the rising spirit of the group. They were ready. Ready to fight. Ready to win. And for the first time in a long time, hope felt real.

The camp had grown quiet, the fire casting long shadows across the determined faces of the group. Adira stood with Vihan and the rest of the team, their minds buzzing with the weight of the new information Jorik and his Intel had brought them.

Jorik, the wiry leader of the Intel, stepped forward, his expression grave. "We don't have the exact blueprint of Arya's Wrath yet, but we've learned where it exists. And that's what we need to get."

Vihan's brow furrowed. "Where?"

Jorik exchanged a glance with his men before answering. "Krizon. Dev's right-hand man. He's the only one who knows where the blueprint is stored—and he's the only one with access to it."

A ripple of tension spread through the group. Krizon was feared for good reason, a man as ruthless and cunning as Dev himself. If he held the blueprint, then getting it wouldn't just be difficult—it would be deadly.

Adira clenched her fists, her mind racing. "So, Krizon has it. But what do we know? Where is he?"

Jorik lowered his voice, leaning in as if even the trees might overhear. "Our sources say he's stationed at the south wing of the palace, overseeing security preparations. The blueprint isn't in his possession, but he knows where it's kept—inside a hidden chamber within the palace. No one gets in or out without Krizon's knowledge. We need him to tell us where the chamber is."

Vihan shook his head, his voice full of skepticism. "So we need to get to Krizon, force him to reveal where the blueprint is stored, and then hope we can retrieve it before Dev catches on?"

Adira's gaze hardened. "We don't have a choice. Without that blueprint, we're flying blind. And if we want to find Arya's Wrath and everything Dev's hoarded, we need to know how to navigate that palace."

The group exchanged uncertain looks, the weight of the challenge sinking in. Krizon wasn't just any soldier. He was Dev's most trusted, a man who would die before betraying his master. But if they could reach him—if they could find a way to turn him—they'd have the upper hand.

Jorik stepped closer, his face grim. "There's one more thing. Krizon is paranoid, always watching his back. He knows people are after Dev's secrets, so he never stays in one place for long. But our latest intel says he's due for a shift change soon, and during that time, he'll be vulnerable. That's when we strike."

Adira nodded, feeling the pressure weigh down on her chest. This was their one chance. If they failed, it wasn't just the blueprint they'd lose—it was their lives.

Vihan exhaled sharply. "So, what's the plan?"

Adira's voice was steady, though her heart pounded in her chest. "We find Krizon. We get him to tell us where the blueprint is hidden. And then… we take it. Once we have it, we'll know how to breach the vault."

She looked around at her team, their faces lit with a mix of determination and fear. They all knew what was at stake, but they also knew this was their only shot.

"This is it," Adira said, her voice stronger now. "We get that blueprint, and we take everything from Dev. This is how we win."

The group fell silent, the fire crackling softly, as the weight of their mission settled over them. They didn't have the blueprint yet, but they knew where it was—and now, all they had to do was survive long enough to get it.

The loss of Kate had shaken them deeply. His leadership and resolve had kept the group united, and now his absence was a painful wound, but they couldn't afford to let it paralyze them. Vihan and the remaining rebels pressed on, their determination only growing stronger. Arya's Wrath—their daring plan to strike at Dev's stronghold—was nearly ready. Each member had a vital role to play in the coming attack, and every step was calculated with precision.

Vihan, however, needed a moment away from the relentless planning. He had taken it upon himself to deliver the news of Kate's death to his family. The journey was somber, and with each step, Vihan felt the weight of grief and responsibility press harder against his chest. As he stood before Kate's grieving family, he realized the full burden of what they were fighting for—justice, freedom, and a future without fear.

Back at the hideout, the mood was tense. The air was thick with anticipation, the rebels sharpening weapons and checking supplies in near silence. Adira, though grieving for Kate, stood strong, her confidence never wavering. She knew they couldn't afford to crumble. With Vihan temporarily gone, she took charge, rallying the others, ensuring they remained focused. She knew the time for mourning would come later—now, they needed to be prepared for the strike that would change everything.

But while Adira's focus was on strengthening their forces, the danger they had always feared was creeping closer. Unbeknownst to them, one of Dev's spies had followed Vihan's trail. The walls of their hideout, once a sanctuary, were no longer as safe as they thought.

CHAPTER 11
Anger, Loss and hope...

Meanwhile, in the heart of Dev's empire, the Chancellor was growing increasingly agitated. Reports of Adira's rising influence disturbed him deeply. He could feel the cracks forming in his control. The hope she inspired had become a thorn in his side. It wasn't just her acts of defiance; it was the idea that the people could stand against him. Dev knew that if she remained free, she would become an even greater symbol of resistance. He issued an urgent order to his generals: Adira had to be captured. And when she was, he would make her execution a spectacle for all to see, a warning to those who dared rise against him.

The rebels, focused on Arya's Wrath, were unaware that Dev's spies had been tracking them for weeks. Their camp had been compromised. On the night before Vihan's return, just as the rebels made their final preparations, Dev's army struck. Explosives shook the camp, and thick smoke poured into the air. The rebels scrambled for cover, but they were unprepared for the force of the assault. Dev's elite troops stormed in, using gas to incapacitate most of the fighters before they even had a chance to react.

Amidst the chaos, Adira tried to rally those still able to fight. But the attack had been swift and brutal. One by one, her comrades fell, until she too was captured, bound, and taken away. Dev's soldiers made quick work of the camp, capturing anyone they found and leaving the once-hidden base in ruins.

The next morning, Vihan returned to find the camp decimated. His heart sank as he surveyed the destruction. There were no signs of life, no clues about what had happened. But soon the truth emerged—Adira and the others had been taken. Dev's army had overwhelmed them, and now she was in his custody. Worse still, Dev had plans for her. He intended to make an example of her in a public execution, hoping to snuff out any lingering hope among the people.

Vihan, devastated by the news, gathered the remaining rebels. The attack on Arya's Wrath, once their focus, now took a backseat. The mission had changed. They would have to act quickly if they wanted to save Adira and stop Dev from using her capture as a way to tighten his grip on the people.

Vihan knew this mission was his last hope. His comrades were captured, locked up in the enemy's most fortified camp, and Adira—his heart clenched—she was there too. She had fought beside him for years, and now, she was in the hands of the enemy. He couldn't let her down.

Through his binoculars, he scanned the camp's perimeter. It was crawling with armed guards, their weapons gleaming under the harsh lights. And there, through the blur of his anxiety, he saw her: Adira, bruised but defiant, chained with their fellow fighters. Rage boiled within him. The enemy didn't know who they were dealing with.

Vihan lowered the binoculars, his heart sinking. His entire team—his closest comrades—were captured, locked inside the enemy camp, surrounded by armed guards. He was the only one left on the outside. The weight of the situation pressed down on him, but he couldn't afford to hesitate. He needed a plan, and fast.

"They're counting on me," he muttered under his breath, tightening his grip on the rifle. His mind raced through the options, but there was no backup, no reinforcements. It was just him against an entire camp of enemy soldiers.

For a brief moment, the reality of the situation hit him hard. They were outnumbered, and now, with his team in chains, they were completely vulnerable. But Vihan had one thing the enemy didn't expect—his sheer, unrelenting determination. If he didn't act, his team wouldn't just be prisoners; they'd be executed by morning.

Taking a deep breath, he focused on the only plan that might work: stealth, speed, and surprise.

As night fell and the camp grew quieter, Vihan moved through the shadows like a ghost. Every step was calculated, his senses heightened. He approached the perimeter slowly, using the cover of darkness. The guards were stationed at regular intervals, patrolling lazily, unaware of the storm brewing in the darkness.

Reaching for his belt, Vihan pulled out a small smoke grenade—his one chance to create enough confusion to make his move. He aimed carefully and tossed it toward the center of the camp. As it clattered to the ground, a thick plume of smoke erupted, covering the area in a dense, choking fog. Shouts and yells rang out as the guards scrambled, disoriented by the sudden chaos.

Vihan wasted no time. He sprinted toward the first guard post, his knife glinting in the faint light. In one swift, silent motion, he dispatched the guard, dragging the body into the shadows before anyone could notice. His movements were fluid, driven by a single purpose—free his team.

Vihan moved swiftly, his eyes locked on the cage where Adira and the others were held. He was close now, just a few more meters. The camp was a war zone, explosions echoing around him, but his focus never wavered.

He reached the cage, crouched low as gunfire erupted around him. With trembling hands, he pulled a lockpick from his belt. The lock was tough, but Vihan's determination was tougher. In seconds, the cage creaked open, and Adira stumbled out, weak but alive.

"You came…" she breathed, her voice barely audible over the chaos.

"Always," Vihan whispered, giving her a nod before turning back to the fight.

But before they could make their escape, the sharp crack of a gunshot split the air. Vihan felt the impact before he heard it—a searing pain tearing through his side. His legs buckled beneath him, and he crashed to the ground, blood spreading across the dirt like a dark stain of defeat.

Adira's scream was lost in the cacophony of war, but her horror was written all over her face. Time slowed as she watched Vihan fall, her mind struggling to process the sight. Her best friend, her rock, the one who had always been there, was now bleeding out in front of her.

"No... no, no, no," she whispered, stumbling toward him. But there was no time.

Vihan's chest heaved, each breath labored, as his hand reached out toward her. "Go..." he rasped, his voice fading. "Get them out..."

Adira stood over Vihan's lifeless body, her heart heavy but her spirit ignited with fury. She quickly discarded his empty gun, knowing she needed something more. Her eyes locked onto a small knife resting on a nearby table. Without hesitation, she lunged for it, her instincts kicking in.

As she grabbed the blade, a soldier lunged at her, but Adira dodged, slamming her elbow into his face. Blood sprayed, and he staggered back, giving her the moment she needed. With the knife in hand, she became a whirlwind of action.

Adira faced the next soldier head-on, slashing at him with deadly precision. Blood splattered across her face as she moved, each strike quick and ruthless. The chaos around her faded; all that mattered was the fight.

Another soldier charged, swinging his rifle at her. Adira ducked and spun, driving the knife deep into his side. He gasped, shock in his eyes, but she didn't look back.

She was a blur, the knife flying through the air as she took down enemy after enemy. With every cut, her confidence grew. Each opponent fell before her, their screams ringing in her ears as she pressed on, drenched in blood yet undeterred.

Then a larger soldier approached, knife raised. Adira met him with fierce determination. They clashed in a brutal struggle, metal on metal, sparks flying. He snarled as he swung wildly, but she was too quick. With a twist of her body, she trapped his arm and drove her knife into his ribs. He collapsed, and she moved on, relentless.

Adira was now soaked in the chaos of battle, her clothes stained red. But instead of slowing her down, it fueled her fire. She moved through the smoke and screams, a warrior on a mission, slicing through the enemy ranks with precision.

Her comrades watched in awe as she fought, inspired by her fearless spirit. With each enemy she took down, their resolve grew stronger. Adira was no longer just a survivor; she was a warrior leading them to victory.

When the last soldier fell, the ground was littered with bodies. Adira stood amidst the chaos, breathing heavily but standing tall. Her face was smeared with blood, her grip tight around the knife that had become an extension of her will.

Her comrades looked at her with newfound respect. She had turned the tide of the battle, proving her strength and determination. Adira wasn't just a fighter; she was a force to be reckoned with, and she had made her mark on this day.

In the aftermath of the brutal battle where Vihan had fallen, Adira stood tall amidst the wreckage, her heart heavy but unyielding. The acrid smell of smoke lingered in the air, mingling with the scent of blood and sweat. Vihan's body lay just a few feet away, a painful reminder of the cost of their rebellion. His death, though devastating, lit a fire in her that could not be quenched.

Adira scanned the faces of her comrades, many of them bloodied and bruised, their eyes full of loss and fear. The silence was deafening, broken only by the crackle of smoldering fires and the distant, fading screams of those who had already fled. But Adira knew this was not the time to succumb to despair. If she let fear take hold, everything Vihan fought for would be lost.

"We cannot allow Vihan's sacrifice to be in vain!" she shouted, her voice cutting through the heavy air. "We have all bled, we have all suffered, but we stand here—unbroken. We are more than survivors. We are warriors!"

Her words rippled through the group, drawing their gaze away from the horror and towards her. "This battle isn't just for us—it's for everyone who has ever been crushed under Dev's regime, for everyone who has been silenced, oppressed, and brutalized. Vihan believed in this cause. He believed in our strength. And we will show them that his belief wasn't misplaced."

Adira's eyes burned with determination as she continued. "They think we are weak. They think fear will stop us. But they don't know what it means to lose everything and still rise. They don't know what it means to fight not just with weapons, but with heart and soul. We are not just soldiers. We are the architects of a new world. And today, we will write the first chapter of its freedom in blood if we must."

Just as the last of her words echoed through the air, a rustle in the underbrush caught her attention. The enemy, lurking in the shadows, had found them again. Before anyone could react, a soldier lunged forward, knife in hand, pressing the cold blade against Adira's throat. The suddenness of the attack sent shockwaves through the group.

Gasps rang out, but Adira remained steady, her eyes fixed on her attacker. The blade was sharp, deadly, but she showed no fear. Her voice, low and cold, challenged the man in front of her. "Do you think killing me will kill this movement? You can cut me down, but you cannot silence the fire we've started. It's bigger than you, bigger than Dev, and bigger than me."

Her comrades froze for a heartbeat, but then, something shifted. The memory of Vihan, his unrelenting spirit, surged through them. They wouldn't let fear paralyze them. One by one, they moved, surrounding the enemy in a surge of raw energy and fury.

"Together, we are stronger than your blades," Adira hissed as she twisted out of the soldier's grasp, her fist connecting with his jaw. "We are the storm you cannot contain."

With a battle cry that echoed across the clearing, her comrades charged. The fight was brutal and swift, fueled by grief, anger, and a sense of righteousness. Steel clashed, fists flew, and the enemy was driven back, overwhelmed by the sheer force of their unity. Adira, though weary, fought with the ferocity of someone who had nothing left to lose and everything to gain. Her strikes were precise, her movements fluid, each swing of her blade a tribute to Vihan's memory.

As the last of the attackers fell, Adira stood in the center of the battlefield, her chest heaving, her heart racing. Blood stained her hands, but in her eyes burned a fire that would not be extinguished. She looked around at her comrades, at the remnants of Dev's men lying defeated on the ground, and knew their fight was far from over. But in this moment, they had won a victory.

They had shown Dev that they were not just fighting for survival—they were fighting for a future. And no matter how many battles he waged, no matter how many lives he took, they would never stop.

Meanwhile, in the shadows of his palace, Dev received the news with a mix of rage and cold satisfaction. He had lost some of his soldiers, but in his eyes, it only confirmed one thing: Adira was dangerous. And dangerous people needed to be dealt with. His lips twisted into a cruel smile as he quietly ordered his army to intensify the search for her.

"Let her have her little victories," he mused. "But when I catch her, I will kill her in front of the very people she claims to fight for. I'll crush their hope, just as I've crushed every rebellion before."

In that moment, both sides steeled themselves for what was to come. Adira, with the weight of Vihan's death fueling her fight, and Dev, with the cold, calculating mind of a tyrant who knew no mercy. The final showdown was inevitable. And the fate of the people hung in the balance.

CHAPTER 12
Smiles of Ruin, Fires of Resolve....

Dev leaned back in his grand chair, his eyes gleaming with a cruel satisfaction as he swirled a glass of wine in his hand. The news of Vihan's death had been delivered to him just moments ago, and it had brightened his mood. Vihan had been a thorn in his side for too long, always scheming, always one step ahead. Now, that was over. The rebellion, as far as Dev was concerned, was crumbling.

A cold smile tugged at the corner of his lips. "One down," he muttered under his breath, his voice thick with arrogance. "And soon, the rest will fall."

From the window of his palace, Dev could see the city below—his city. His kingdom. Everything was under his control, bound by fear and his iron fist. The people trembled at the mere mention of his name, and Vihan's death would serve as yet another reminder of his untouchable power. The rebellion's leader was gone, and without him, they would scatter like frightened mice.

But Dev wasn't done. Not yet. Adira was still out there, somewhere, plotting. He could sense her anger, her pain. And it delighted him. He relished the idea of breaking her—destroying her hope just as he had destroyed Vihan.

"I want her found," Dev said sharply, turning to his captain of the guard. "Alive, for now. She needs to see what happens to her people when they dare to stand against me. Kill the rest of her crew. Make sure she hears every scream, every death. Let her know that her resistance is futile."

As the captain left to carry out his orders, Dev allowed himself a moment of smug triumph. He had crushed countless rebellions before, and this would be no different. Adira was just another pawn in his game, and soon she would fall, like all the others.

Adira knelt beside Vihan's body, her heart aching with a grief so deep it nearly paralyzed her. His blood still stained her hands, his face pale and lifeless. But beneath that grief, a storm was brewing—a rage that threatened to consume her entirely. Vihan had died in her arms, and she had been powerless to stop it.

The brutal truth of his death had hit her like a hammer, and now, as she stared at his motionless form, that pain transformed into something else—something fierce, unforgiving.

In her mind, she could already see Dev's smirk, hear his arrogant laughter. She knew him well enough to know he'd be celebrating this victory, reveling in the torment he had caused her. Vihan's death had been a calculated move, a message sent directly to her: *You are next.*

But Dev had made a mistake—a fatal one. In killing Vihan, he had given Adira all the reason she needed to keep fighting. Not for survival, not for freedom alone, but for vengeance. For justice. Vihan's blood would not be spilled in vain.

As the rebels gathered around her, some murmuring prayers, others struggling to contain their own emotions, Adira stood up. Her hands clenched into fists, her body trembling with barely contained fury.

"We strike now," she said, her voice sharp, commanding.

Vikram, still visibly shaken by Vihan's death, looked at her with wide eyes. "Adira, we're not ready. Dev's forces are—"

"We strike now," Adira repeated, cutting him off. "Every minute we wait is another life lost. Vihan's death won't slow Dev down. He's already moving against us, tightening his grip. But we'll break him. We'll take down Krizon and burn Dev's war machine to the ground."

Her words hung in the air, thick with the promise of violence and retribution. There was no fear in her eyes now, only resolve. Dev had declared war, and Adira was ready to answer that call with fire.

Dev, meanwhile, was enjoying the fruits of his brutality. Reports were coming in from all over—rebel cells being crushed, civilians cowering in fear. His soldiers had dragged out several of Adira's remaining crew members, executing them in public squares, making examples of them.

In his mind, Dev could see Adira watching as her friends were slaughtered one by one. He imagined her anguish, her helplessness, and it filled him with glee.

"She's running out of places to hide," Dev said to his advisors, his voice cold and triumphant. "We'll drag her out of whatever hole she's hiding in, and when we do, she'll beg for mercy."

He leaned forward, his eyes narrowing as he imagined the final moment—Adira, broken and bloodied at his feet. "And I'll give her none."

Adira, on the other hand, was anything but broken. With every brutal report of her crew's deaths, her fury grew. She knew what Dev was doing—he wanted to break her spirit, to crush her before she had a chance to fight back. But it wasn't working. If anything, it was giving her more strength.

They had tracked Krizon's fortress, the heart of Dev's operations, and Adira had made up her mind. There would be no more waiting, no more hiding. This was the moment she had been building towards, the moment to strike back, not just for freedom, but for Vihan, for all those Dev had crushed under his boot.

"We'll get that blueprint," she said, her voice low but filled with steel. "And we'll make Dev pay for every single death."

The rebels around her, still shaken, nodded in agreement. They could see it now—the fire in her eyes, the unstoppable force she had become. Adira wasn't just fighting for their cause anymore. She was fighting for vengeance, for retribution.

And Dev? He didn't know it yet, but his days of tyranny were numbered.

The battle was coming. And Adira was ready.

CHAPTER 13
Last Stand: Fight or Fall

Adira had hit a wall. For weeks, they had been tracking every lead, every whisper about Dev's ammunition palace. But all trails led to one hard truth: the blueprint and all the crucial information about the building were in the hands of Krizon, Dev's most trusted ally. Krizon's home wasn't just a mansion—it was a fortress in itself, built like a personal vault, filled with traps, and patrolled by elite guards. And no one had ever broken in and lived to tell the tale.

Adira sat in the dim light of their hideout, staring at the scattered intel on the table. Nira stood nearby, sharpening her blade, while Rohan studied floor plans of Krizon's estate. Vikram leaned against the wall, arms crossed, watching the team quietly.

"We can't do this the way we did the last job," Rohan said, breaking the silence. "Krizon's place isn't a normal target. It's a death trap. We can't just walk in and grab the blueprint. It's locked deep inside his personal study, probably hidden in a safe, and from what I've heard, Krizon himself is almost never far from it."

Adira nodded slowly. "Then we'll have to make sure Krizon is nowhere near that safe when we take it."

Nira looked up. "You want to draw him out?"

"Exactly," Adira replied. "But first, we need to know how to get inside without setting off every alarm."

Rohan zoomed in on the estate's layout. "There's one way in that's not covered by his usual security—an old servant tunnel under the building. I managed to find a vague mention of it in some old city records. It hasn't been used in years, but if we can find the entrance, we could slip in undetected."

"That's a start," Vikram said. "But how do we deal with Krizon?"

Adira smiled slightly, her mind racing. "We'll bait him. If we can create enough chaos in one of his business fronts, he'll have no choice but to leave his estate and handle it personally. He doesn't trust anyone to take care of his money."

The plan came together fast. The team set a small fire at one of Krizon's warehouses on the outskirts of the city, destroying a shipment of valuable contraband. It wasn't enough to bring his empire down, but it was enough to make him furious. As they had hoped, Krizon left his estate, taking most of his top guards with him, racing to salvage what he could from the burning warehouse.

As soon as he was gone, Adira and her team made their move.

Under the cover of darkness, they found the old tunnel entrance, hidden beneath overgrown weeds and rubble at the edge of the estate grounds. It was narrow, damp, and smelled of decay, but it led them straight under the mansion and into the wine cellar. From there, they moved quietly, keeping low as they navigated the grand halls of Krizon's home.

The mansion was as lavish as it was secure—crystal chandeliers hung from the ceiling, reflecting the moonlight through large windows. The floors were polished marble, and the walls were lined with rare paintings and expensive décor. But the beauty didn't distract them; they knew what was lurking behind every corner—hidden passages, secret doors, and the few guards Krizon had left behind.

Nira led the way, slipping through the shadows, her every step calculated and silent. Rohan followed, using a small vial of oil to silence the creaky hinges of doors they passed. Vikram stayed at the back, ready to engage if things went sideways.

Finally, they reached Krizon's study—a grand, oak-paneled room with a huge fireplace and bookshelves that stretched to the ceiling. At the far end of the room was the safe, hidden behind an elaborate painting of a battle scene. Adira's eyes narrowed. It wasn't just an ordinary safe; it was custom-made, likely by one of the best in the world, just like the vault they would face in Dev's palace.

"We've got five minutes, tops," Rohan whispered, glancing at the hourglass he carried. "Krizon's going to realize something's off soon."

Nira moved swiftly to the painting, her fingers tracing the edges until she found the hidden latch. With a soft click, the painting swung open, revealing the safe. The room seemed to hold its breath as Adira stepped forward, her tools ready. She began to work on the lock, her hands steady but her mind racing.

Outside the study, the faint sound of footsteps echoed through the hallways. Vikram tensed, his hand gripping the hilt of his sword. The guards were closer than they had anticipated. He signaled to Rohan, who nodded and moved to the door, ready to hold it shut if necessary.

Adira moved swiftly to the safe, her heart racing. She had come prepared, knowing this would be the toughest lock she'd faced yet. It wasn't about brute strength —it required precision. She carefully examined the mechanism, her fingers moving with practiced ease. Every click and shift of the dials felt like a countdown in her head.

Behind her, Nira and Vikram kept watch, ears straining for any sign of approaching guards. The tension was suffocating.

Sweat trickled down Adira's forehead as she turned the final dial. Her pulse quickened. One wrong move and the safe would be impossible to open. But after what felt like an eternity, she heard it—a soft click.

The safe door swung open, revealing stacks of documents, gold bars, and—there it was—the blueprint.

Adira quickly pulled it out, unrolling it to reveal the detailed layout of Dev's ammunition palace. Every room, every security measure was there, but most importantly, it showed the hidden vault, the heart of Dev's empire. Alongside the blueprint were several folders, packed with information on Dev's operations—locations, weapon stockpiles, and financial records.

"We've got it," Adira whispered. "Everything we need."

Suddenly, an alarm blared, cutting through the silence.

"They know we're here!" Nira hissed, pulling her knife from its sheath.

"We're out of time," Rohan said, stuffing the remaining documents into a bag. "We've got to move!"

The mansion came alive with the sound of guards storming in. Adira shoved the blueprint into her jacket and turned to run, but not before a gunshot rang out. A bullet grazed Vikram's shoulder, spinning him around. He grunted in pain but didn't slow down.

"Let's go!" Adira yelled, throwing a smoke grenade behind them to cover their escape.

They dashed back through the mansion, hearts pounding, bullets flying past them as they sprinted for the tunnel. The guards were closing in, their shouts echoing through the halls, but they reached the tunnel entrance just in time, disappearing into the darkness.

They didn't stop running until they were clear of the estate, breathing hard as they slipped into the night. They had the blueprint. They had the intel. And now, with Krizon's estate in chaos, they were one step closer to bringing down Dev's empire.

Adira glanced at the folded map in her hand, feeling the weight of the battle to come. This was just the beginning.

As Adira carefully rolled up the blueprint and stashed it inside her jacket, a faint sound caught her attention. It was subtle, almost imperceptible-the creak of a floorboard outside Krizon's study.

"Wait, she whispered, holding up her hand to silence the team. The crew froze, tension crackling through the air. Vikram's eyes darted toward the door, his muscles tensing, ready to spring into action.

For a moment, there was nothing but silence. And then, the unmistakable click of a weapon being cocked

"Move!" Adira hissed, just as the door to the study burst open.

Krizon's men stormed in, guns raised, their black combat gear blending into the shadows. Adira dropped to the floor just as bullets whizzed overhead shattering the chandelier and sending glass raining down like deadly confetti. Nira dove behind a nearby bookshelf, her knife already in hand, while Vikram drew his pistol and returned fire.

"Get the hell out of here!" Vikram barked, covering Adira as she scrambled behind the desk, the blueprint still clutched to her chest.

Two of Krizon's men advanced quickly, their boots pounding against the stone floor. One of them locked eyes on Rohan, who was crouched low near the estate's main gate, frantically working to dismantle the heavy chains and complex locks that barred their escape. Rohan was exposed, out in the open, his fingers trembling as he fumbled with the tools they had scavenged.

The sound of approaching footsteps grew louder. Time was running out. The guards weren't just armed with brute strength—they carried the authority of Krizon, a man known for his merciless enforcement of order. Rohan's hands moved faster, sweat dripping down his brow, knowing that even a second's hesitation could spell doom for them all.

His allies were fighting on the far side of the courtyard, drawing attention away from him, but the two guards were too close. There was nowhere to hide.

Nira acted without thinking. With lightning speed, she hurled her knife across the room, the blade slicing through the air and embedding itself into the neck of the closest guard. He dropped instantly, blood pooling beneath him. The second guard hesitated just long enough for Vikram to get a clean shot. A single round to the chest, and he was down.

But more were coming

The hallway outside echoed with the heavy footsteps of reinforcements. Krizon's men weren't amateurs-they moved with military precision, flanking the study from both sides, cutting off any chance of escape

"Rohan!" she shouted over the clamor of clashing swords and shouts.

"Can you find a way to silence the alarms?"

"Working on it!" Rohan snapped, his hands frantically rummaging through his satchel for a method to block the warning bells. "But they've set up a backup signal—it won't hold them off for long!"

"We don't have long!" Vikram growled, swinging his blade to fend off the advancing guards. "We need to move, now!"

Suddenly, a smoke bomb was tossed into the room, landing at Adira's feet.

"Shit!" she screamed, instinctively covering her face and ducking just as the device erupted. The air filled with acrid smoke, swirling and thickening around her. For a few moments, chaos reigned. Her vision blurred, the sounds of battle muffled by the haze, and her heart raced in her chest.

As she staggered back, coughing and disoriented, she felt Rohan grab her arm. "This way!" he urged, pulling her toward a shadowy exit. Adira squinted through the smoke, the figures of guards moving like wraiths, and she could barely make out Vikram fighting fiercely against their encroaching numbers.

"Go!" Vikram shouted, his voice strained. "I'll hold them off!"

"No!" Adira yelled, her resolve hardening. "We're not leaving you behind!"

In that moment of clarity, the three of them locked eyes. They were a team, forged in the fire of countless battles. With a shared nod, they pressed forward, ready to face whatever came next together.

Through the disorienting haze, she saw more guards rushing in, their shadows dancing in the smoke. She blinked hard, trying to clear her head, just as one of the men lunged at her with a blade. Instinct took over. She ducked, narrowly avoiding the knife, and drove her elbow into his ribs with brutal force. He staggered back, but before he could recover, Adira grabbed a broken shard of glass from the shattered chandelier and slashed it across his face.

The guard screamed and dropped to the floor, clutching his bleeding face.

Vikram was on his last clip, each shot precise and deadly as he took down one guard after another. But there were too many of them. Even Nira, with her speed and deadly precision, was starting to slow under the relentless assault.

Vikram was on his last clip, each shot precise and deadly as he took down one guard after another. But there were too many of them. Even Nira, with her speed and deadly precision, was starting to slow under the relentless assault.

"Rohan, NOW!" Adira yelled, grabbing his arm as another round of bullets shattered the desk they were hiding behind.

"I'm in!" Rohan shouted, just as the alarms cut off abruptly. The estate fell into a strange, tense silence-no blaring alarms, just the sound of distant shouts and gunfire

"Move!" Adira ordered, pulling her team toward the secret tunnel.

But just as they made it to the doorway, another squad of Krizon's men appeared in the hall, blocking their escape. One of the men-a towering brute with a scar running down his face-stepped forward, grinning. He leveled a shotgun directly at Adira's chest,

There was no time to think.

Vikram acted first, lunging at the brute just as the shotgun fired. The blast echoed through the narrow hall, deafening in its intensity.

Vikram slammed into the man with all his weight, driving him back into the wall as the shotgun blast went wide, tearing chunks out of the ceiling instead of hitting Adira.

Adira didn't waste a second. She sprinted toward the tunnel, dragging Rohan behind her while Nira covered their rear, her knives flashing in the dim light.

Vikram struggled with the brute, their fight brutal and raw. The guard was strong—too strong—but Vikram was faster. He ducked under a wild punch, twisted the man's arm behind his back, and slammed his head into the wall with a sickening crack.

"Go!" Vikram shouted, blood running down his face as he staggered toward the tunnel.

The crew bolted through the narrow passageway, their hearts racing, knowing they had barely escaped. The tunnel was dark, the only sound their ragged breathing as they ran, adrenaline pumping through their veins. Behind them, they could hear the shouts of Krizon's men closing in. They were still in danger, still a heartbeat away from being caught or killed.

But as they reached the exit and burst into the cool night air, they knew they had done it. The blueprint was in their hands, and Krizon had no idea just how much damage they could now do.

Adira glanced at the rolled-up map tucked safely in her jacket. It had been a close call-too close. But they had what they needed.

Dev's empire was going to fall, and they were the ones who would bring it down.

"We made it," Nira breathed, clutching her side where a bullet had grazed her.

"For now, Adira said, her eyes narrowing as she looked back at the mansion. "But this war is just getting started."

Adira crouched on the rooftop, her eyes locked on the imposing structure below—the ammunition building. Inside it lay a treasure trove of weapons and wealth, enough to cripple the corrupt regime of Dev. But her true obstacle was not the heavily armed guards or the layers of surveillance—it was the locker. The world's safest, created by one of history's greatest locksmiths, Viraaj Kaal.

The locker had a backstory steeped in tragedy and determination. Viraaj, once a simple blacksmith in a remote village, was a man of unparalleled talent. He could forge anything with his hands, and no lock had ever eluded his skill. His life was humble but filled with love. He had a wife, Meera, and a young daughter, Arya. They were his world.

But the peace of his life was shattered when Dev's forces raided his village. Looking for a skilled locksmith, Dev's men threatened his family if he didn't comply. Viraaj refused. The price for his defiance was Arya's life. She was taken from him in front of his eyes. Crushed, Viraaj fell to his knees, forced to craft locks for Dev's war empire.

Consumed by grief and anger, Viraaj vowed to create a lock that could never be opened—a final testament to the daughter he lost. The masterpiece he forged, known as "Arya's Wrath," became the locker that held Dev's most prized possessions. A work of unmatched precision, it was said to be unbreakable. Only Viraaj knew the secret to unlocking it, but he disappeared soon after finishing his creation, vanishing into the mists of history.

As Adira gazed down at the structure, she knew the emotional weight behind her mission. Arya's Wrath wasn't just a vault; it was a symbol of pain, betrayal, and the unyielding love of a father. To break it, she would need more than skill—she'd need to honor the tragedy that forged it.

And so, she prepared herself, knowing the true battle wasn't just against Dev, but against a father's eternal legacy, sealed in the heart of an unbreakable lock.

The night was cold, the air heavy with tension as Adira and her crew crept toward the ammunition building. They were the best at what they did—each one had a role to play. Rohan, the tech genius, had already hacked the outer security. Nira, the stealth expert, was a ghost, moving ahead without a sound. Vikram, the muscle of the group, stayed close, ready for any fight that might come their way. But Adira's mind was fixed on one thing: the locker. The impenetrable vault at the heart of the building, crafted by the legendary locksmith, Viraaj Kaal.

As they reached the perimeter, Adira gave the signal. "Stay sharp. Once we're in, we've got ten minutes. No mistakes."

They slipped through the fence and into the shadows, moving silently to the vent system. Crawling through the narrow ducts, they could hear the guards beneath them, their heavy boots echoing through the hallways. Every creak of the metal vent felt like it could give them away. Hearts pounded, but they stayed focused.

Finally, they dropped into the central chamber. The vault loomed ahead of them—a massive, steel structure surrounded by walls of concrete. Rohan rushed to the nearby terminal, his fingers flying over the keyboard.

"I'm in," he said, but his voice was tense. "I can't shut off the motion sensors. Once we open the vault, we have five minutes."

"Then we work fast," Adira said, her eyes on the vault. She knew the real challenge wasn't just getting inside. It was opening that locker.

They pushed through the doors and entered the heart of the building. The room was dimly lit, but in the center stood the locker—Arya's Wrath. It was huge, covered in intricate carvings, the kind that looked ancient yet alive, pulsing with energy. The legend behind it was real. Viraaj Kaal had crafted it in honor of his daughter, Arya, who was taken from him by Dev's men. The lock was not just steel and gears—it was a symbol of his pain and vengeance.

Adira swallowed hard. She had studied the lock for months, but now, standing in front of it, she felt the weight of the man's grief pressing down on her. This was no ordinary vault.

Suddenly, alarms blared.

"They know we're here!" Nira whispered sharply, her gun ready.

"No time for quiet anymore," Vikram growled. "Get that locker open."

Gunshots echoed from the hallway as the first wave of guards approached. Rohan and Nira fired back, holding the line. Vikram sealed the door, but it wouldn't hold for long.

Adira's hands were steady as she approached the locker, though her heart was racing. The dials were cold and smooth under her fingers. She turned the first one slowly, feeling the gears click beneath her touch. Each movement had to be perfect—one wrong twist could lock it forever. Or worse, set off the trap Inside.

"Adira, hurry up!" Vikram shouted, shoving a heavy desk against the door as the guards pounded against it.

"I'm almost there!" she snapped, her focus razor-sharp. She turned the second dial. The guards outside were getting closer, their shouts growing louder. Rohan and Nira laid down cover fire, but they were outnumbered. Bullets flew, sparks bouncing off the steel walls.

Another click. The third dial fell into place. Adira wiped the sweat from her brow, her breath quick and shallow. She was running out of time. The door was about to give in.

"We can't hold them much longer!" Nira yelled, blood running down her arm from a close shot.

Adira twisted the final dial. Silence. Then—a soft hiss. The locker opened.

Inside were piles of cash, weapons, and a small, gleaming key. The key to the deeper vaults of Dev's empire—the real target of their mission.

"Got it!" Adira shouted, grabbing the key.

"Let's move!" Vikram tossed a smoke grenade, filling the room with thick clouds. In the confusion, the crew slipped out, vanishing into the night as guards swarmed the building.

As they disappeared into the shadows, Adira clutched the key, her heart still pounding. They had done it. The impossible locker had been cracked, and with it, they now had the means to take down Dev's empire piece by piece. But this was only the beginning.

Somewhere, Adira could almost feel the presence of Viraaj and his daughter, Arya—their pain, their revenge. This wasn't just about the mission anymore. It was about justice. And it wasn't over yet.

Adira's hands trembled as she stood before Arya's Wrath. The locker loomed like a monster, its gears whispering a deadly promise. She knew every inch of this lock, had studied it endlessly, but now, under the crushing pressure of time and chaos, it seemed foreign, like it was alive and daring her to fail.

Gunfire cracked behind her. The guards were closing in fast, their shouts growing louder, closer. Rohan and Nira were pinned down, bullets sparking off metal walls as they returned fire. The reinforced door buckled under the weight of the guards trying to break through.

"Adira, now or never!" Vikram shouted, slamming his back against the door, trying to buy her more time. The hinges groaned, ready to give way. One more hit, and the guards would flood in.

Her fingers danced across the dials, twisting them carefully, feeling for the subtle clicks. Each turn sent a jolt of panic through her veins. One wrong move and it could all end in disaster. She was on her fourth dial, sweat dripping into her eyes. Her vision blurred as she focused.

Suddenly, a loud bang. The door behind her cracked open, just enough for a guard to shove his gun through. Vikram slammed the door shut, but not before a round fired, grazing his shoulder. He grunted in pain, blood soaking his shirt.

"We're out of time!" Rohan shouted as he emptied his clip, taking out two more guards. Nira was bleeding from her leg, but she kept shooting, refusing to go down.

Adira swallowed her fear, forcing herself to stay steady. She twisted the final dial. Her heart pounded in her chest, so loud she could barely hear anything else. She held her breath.

Click.

The locker hissed open, the heavy door swinging outward with a soft metallic groan. Inside lay mountains of cash, rows of high-tech weapons, and crates of ammunition.

"We got it!" Adira screamed, grabbing as much as she could. Rohan and Nira rushed over, stuffing bags with money and weapons, moving faster than they ever had before.

But the door behind them exploded open. Guards stormed in, rifles raised.

"Go, go, go!" Vikram shouted, pulling out a smoke grenade and tossing it into the room. The chamber filled with thick, choking smoke. Adira could barely see through the haze, but she kept moving, her heart racing as bullets whizzed past her head.

They were just feet from escaping when a guard appeared in the smoke, his gun aimed directly at her. Time seemed to slow. She froze, staring down the barrel of his weapon, knowing she had only seconds left.

But before he could fire, Vikram tackled him, slamming him to the ground with a brutal force. "Get out, now!" Vikram roared, as the rest of the guards poured into the room.

Adira grabbed the last crate of weapons and sprinted toward the exit, her lungs burning, her legs shaking. The crew barely made it out, dodging bullets that seemed to tear through the air just inches from them. They ran into the night, slipping through the shadows as alarms blared and chaos erupted behind them.

They had escaped by a thread—bloodied, bruised, but alive. And they had it all—the money, the weapons, and the key to Dev's downfall.

As they disappeared into the darkness, Adira could hardly believe they had made it. One second later, and they all would have been dead.

The night air crackled with tension as Adira's team advanced toward

Chancellor Dev's heavily fortified palace, their hearts pounding with a mix of fear and determination. They had already executed a daring raid on Dev's secret safe, liberating a trove of wealth and advanced weaponry. But their mission extended far beyond this single stronghold. Across the city, other teams were poised to capture Dev's army heads and loyal supporters at various strategic locations. Each thread of their plan was interwoven; if one snapped, the entire resistance would unravel.

"Stick to the plan," Adira reminded her team as they crouched in the shadows, She scanned the towering walls of the palace, illuminated by flickering torches. "We need to create a diversion to draw out his guards.".

Meanwhile, in a nearby warehouse, Kael led another team. "We hit them hard and fast," he instructed, his eyes narrowed with focus. "If we can cut off their supply lines, we'll cripple Dev's forces. They knew the stakes: if they didn't succeed, Dev's reinforcements could turn the tide of battle in an instant.

As Adira's team initiated their assault, explosives set at key points around the palace detonated, sending shockwaves through the night. The guards, caught off guard, scrambled to respond, their confusion palpable. Adira's fighters surged forward, moving with calculated precision. They engaged in fierce hand-to-hand combat, using the weapons they had seized to turn the tide in their favor.

At the same time, Kael's team burst into the warehouse, catching Dev's supply officers by surprise. The chaos was electric; they moved like shadows, incapacitating guards and seizing crates of ammunition. The clock was ticking. And they had to hold their positions until Adira's team could join them.

"Push through!" Adira urged, adrenaline fueling her as they reached a fortified checkpoint. Just as they prepared to advance, reinforcements from Dev's elite guard arrived, a line of fierce defenders. The air thickened with tension as both sides prepared for an explosive confrontation.

"Regroup!" Adira shouted, her voice cutting through the noise. They formed a defensive line, determined to hold their ground. With each passing second, she stole glances at her wristwatch counting down the moments until Kael's diversion would create a critical opportunity.

In the warehouse, Kael detonated explosives, a thunderous blast resonating through the city, creating a massive distraction that sent guards rushing away from the palace. "Now! This is our chance!" Adira yelled, leading her fighters through the gap, heart racing as they stormed the inner chamber of the palace.

Inside, the atmosphere crackled with tension. They faced Chancellor Dev, flanked by his most loyal supporters. Fury etched on their faces. "You think you can overthrow me?" Dev sneered, raising his weapon, his voice dripping with disdain.

"Your time is over, Dev!" Adira declared, her heart pounding in her chest. The fight erupted, chaos swirling as the resistance clashed with Dev's guards The room transformed into a battlefield, every blow reverberating with the weight of their struggle and the lives at stake.

As they fought, Adira felt the pressure mounting. Every second counted; they needed to eliminate Dev and dismantle his command structure before his forces could regroup. The fate of the resistance hung in the balance.

With each strike, she channeled the pain and suffering of those who had suffered under Dev's tyranny. She pushed forward, adrenaline surging as she engaged in a brutal dance of combat. In the midst of the chaos, she caught a glimpse of Kael's team through the palace windows. Their success depended on hers; if they faltered now, everything would unravel.

With a final, decisive blow, Adira disarmed Dev, standing over him as the last of his guards fell. "This is for everyone you've oppressed," she said, her voice steady, filled with the righteous fury of those who had suffered in silence for far too long.

As the resistance fought valiantly to secure their victory, Kael and his team were not finished. They continued their mission across the city, capturing Dev's key supporters, ensuring that no one would be left to rally against the uprising.

Adira felt the weight of the moment heavy in the air. If they missed this opportunity, the resistance could collapse, and the fight for freedom would be lost. The threads of fate hung by a delicate balance, and she was determined to seize this chance, ready to forge a new future for her people. The battle for liberation was only just beginning.

CHAPTER 14
A New Dawn: The End of Oppression

Adira stood before Chancellor Dev, her sword glinting in the flickering torchlight. He was a figure of cold authority, reminiscent of history's most formidable leaders, and his presence filled the room with an oppressive weight

The dim light of the war room flickered, casting shadows on the cracked walls, as Adira stood face-to-face with Chancellor Dev. The air was thick with tension, the quiet outside betrayed only by the distant sounds of rebellion brewing in the streets. The silence between them was as dangerous as the storm raging outside.

Dev, leaning back in his seat, exhaled slowly. "You think you've won something, Adira?" His voice was low, calculated. "You think this is about freedom? "My father inherited the throne when this land was still clinging to the idea of kingship, of bloodlines shaping nations. For me, the throne isn't just a seat of power—it's my birthright," he began, his voice laced with both pride and bitterness. "He believed that giving power to the people—*true* power—would somehow elevate them, change their lives, and fuel their growth. He thought that by giving the poor the means to choose their leaders, we could usher in an era of equality."

He stopped, turning his sharp gaze to Adira, his voice dripping with disdain. "But do you know what that did? It gave them a taste of control they were never prepared for. My father, in his idealism, underestimated human nature. He thought they would rise above their hunger, their petty desires, and work for the collective good. But instead? They sold their votes, their loyalty, for scraps. Greed overtook them before any notion of freedom could bloom."

Adira's eyes flared with anger, but she kept her voice calm. "That's because men like you thrive on their division. You exploit their fear to keep them weak."

Dev chuckled, the sound dark and hollow. "Fear? Fear is the only thing that unites them now. You believe in freedom, but look what freedom got them—nothing but chaos and corruption. Even your precious Minervan, a man you trusted like a brother—what did he choose when I gave him the option? Power. Not freedom. He was just like the rest, drunk on the illusion of control."

Adira's fists clenched. "Minervan was a traitor. He doesn't represent the people. There are others who still believe, who still fight for something greater than themselves."

Dev's voice dropped, filled with contempt. "And you think they're different? You think they'll stay pure once they have a taste of power? The truth is, Adira, they're all the same. You can call it 'freedom,' but people will always choose what benefits them most. My father's mistake was trusting them. I won't make the same error."

Adira's gaze sharpened. "Your father gave them a chance. You took that away and turned them into slaves. You've ruled through fear, but fear can only last so long. Once they see hope—once they believe in something greater than you—they'll rise up."

Dev stood, his face inches from hers now, the weight of his presence suffocating. "Hope?" He hissed. "Hope is a flicker in the dark, easily snuffed out. Fear, though—fear endures. It's the foundation of control, the only thing that keeps order. Without fear, they'd tear each other apart. They need someone like me, someone who understands that. You think you can kill me and free them, but you don't understand—you can't kill what I am."

Adira's brow furrowed, confusion briefly flickering across her face. "What are you talking about?"

Dev's lips twisted into a grim smile. "Even if you strike me down, I'll still be alive—in the greed, the corruption, the hunger for power that exists in every human heart. You'll see it in those around you, in those you trust most. "Power" itself is the corruption. It's not the men who wield it—it's the nature of the beast. Even your beloved 'freedom fighters' will one day betray you, just like Minervan."

Adira's heart raced, but her voice was steady. "I'm not like you, Dev. And neither are the people I fight for. We still believe in something better. We're not ruled by greed."

Dev's voice turned mocking, his words cutting deep. "You're so naive. 'It is not heroes who make history, but history which makes heroes,' as wise man once said. You think you're the hero here? You think you'll change the world? No, Adira, the world changes you. Power corrupts everything, no matter how noble you think you are. You'll take the throne, and you'll face the same choices I did. And when you do, you'll find that fear is the only tool that works. You'll need to control them, and when that day comes, you'll become exactly what you hate."

Adira's breath caught in her throat, his words gnawing at the edge of her resolve. But she shook her head, her voice growing fiercer. "I won't become like you. I'm fighting for a world where people don't have to live in fear."

Dev stepped closer, his voice a sinister whisper. "You think I like this? You think I enjoy ruling through fear? No. I do it because it's necessary. My father's dream failed because he trusted people to do the right thing. But people don't do the right thing. They're greedy, selfish, short-sighted. Even now, in the name of your precious 'freedom,' there's betrayal brewing around you. Mark my words, Adira, the moment you take control, they'll betray you, just like they betrayed me."

Adira's heart hammered in her chest, the weight of his words heavy, but she refused to break. "That's where you're wrong. People can change. They just need a chance, a leader who believes in them. You've crushed their spirit, but I'm going to show them what it means to be free."

Dev laughed bitterly. "Free? From what? From me? You think you'll be some kind of savior, but once you're in power, you'll see the truth. The same people who chant your name today will turn on you tomorrow. Power corrupts, Adira, and no one is immune. You can kill me, but that won't end the corruption—it lives in all of them."

His eyes locked onto hers, his voice dropping to a chilling calm. "Go ahead, kill me. Take the throne. But know this—you'll never truly be free of me. Fear, greed, power… these are eternal. And when your so-called 'freedom' falls apart, and the people turn on you, remember this moment. Remember that I warned you."

Adira's grip tightened on her weapon, her voice breaking through the tension. "I don't need to remember anything you say, Dev. Because I'm not fighting for power. I'm fighting for people who deserve a chance to live without fear. You may be right that power corrupts, but I won't be the one holding it. The people will."

Dev's smile was a cold, lifeless thing. "You'll see, Adira. You'll see that in the end, fear will always win. Take my life, but know that you're not just killing a man. You're killing the last person who understands the truth."

Adira raised her weapon, her resolve unwavering, even as his final words hung in the air like a curse.

Adira's heart raced as his words sank in Memories of her childhood struggles and the suffering of her people flooded her mind. Had he truly been the necessary evil, the dark architect of her rise? The very thought shook her to the core.

"Your reign has bred fear, Dev!" she countered, her voice steady despite the turmoil within. "You've kept them in chains under the guise of order, but they need hope, not tyranny.

Dev stepped closer, his eyes narrowing "Hope? You think that will protect them? They will corrupt this country again, and the chaos will be worse than before. I made this place clean! You are naïve to think that kindness will win over power.

Adira felt the weight of his challenge. He was right in some ways; the scars of corruption ran deep. "But what is your solution? To rule forever through fear? You've shown them the worst of humanity, and that's what they will emulate if you remain.

His expression hardened, but beneath it, she saw a flicker of uncertainty."The reality is that I control the chaos. Without me, you'll unleash a flood of corrupt leaders, each one worse than the last. You think you can trust them to govern themselves?"

Adira hesitated, torn between the fear of the chaos he threatened and the desire for a just world. "If 1 kill you, it won't be for power. It will be to break the cycle of tyranny.

Dev's voice dropped, almost pleading "And who will you replace me with? A puppet? A hero who will falter? The truth is, I am the lesser evil. My power keeps the darkness at bay:'

Adira stood at the threshold of power, the heavy air between her and Dev thick with unresolved tension. The room seemed to shrink around them as the fate of a nation balanced precariously on her next words. Dev, the long-reigning chancellor who had justified his rule through chaos and fear, now stood before her, no longer invincible. His steely mask cracked, and for a moment, Adira could sense something deeper in him—a fear he could not admit.

"You're right," Adira said, her voice steady but fierce, surprising herself with the resolve behind her words. "Power corrupts. No one is immune. But I'm not here to pretend I'm above it. I'm here to prove that I won't fall like the others. I will take the throne, Dev. Not because I want it, but because the people deserve to see that leadership can be different. That I can be different."

Dev's eyes narrowed. "You think the throne will bend to your will? That the moment you take it, you won't become what I am? Or worse?"

"Maybe," she admitted, her gaze unwavering. "But if I don't try, we're all lost. And I won't rule through fear. I don't need to destroy you to rise. But I won't forgive you either. You've done too much damage."

She watched as Dev's facade crumbled further, but he wasn't finished yet. A dark smile tugged at the corners of his mouth, though his eyes revealed the uncertainty of a man who no longer trusted his own control.

"You may be right, Adira," he said, his voice quieter now, almost resigned. "But you're not ready for what comes next. You've only seen the tip of the iceberg. I kept the worst of them at bay. The real monsters, the ones you can't see—those are the ones who will come for you when I'm gone. The greedy, the desperate, the ones who wear the mask of loyalty but dream of power. When they see you rise, they will tear you apart. And the people..."

Adira's heart raced, Dev's words hanging in the air like a noose tightening around her choices. "And the people..." He paused, his voice dripping with the weight of years spent controlling them. "The people will look to you, Adira, but they don't want freedom. They want security. And when they see you stumble, even for a moment, they'll turn on you. They'll demand a ruler like me again. One who knows how to keep them safe, how to control the chaos."

Adira clenched her fists, fighting back the urge to respond with the anger boiling inside her. Dev was trying to trap her, make her doubt everything she stood for. But in his desperation, there was a truth she couldn't ignore: the people had been molded by his fear for so long, they might not know how to rise without it.

"I understand now," she said, her voice measured. "You never believed in them. You saw their flaws, their fears, and you used that to keep them in line. But what if you're wrong, Dev? What if they can be more than you think? What if I can lead them without becoming you?"

His expression hardened, but she caught the flicker of uncertainty behind his eyes.

"You think I want to hold onto this forever?" he shot back, bitterness seeping through his calm exterior. "I carry this burden because no one else can. You think I haven't considered stepping aside? Every time I've thought of it, I saw what would come. The chaos, the bloodshed, the greed that would rise. The power I hold isn't just for me—it's to protect them from themselves."

Adira stepped closer, her voice softer now, but laced with conviction. "And yet, you're the one who fostered that very greed. You've shown them the worst of themselves and given them nothing better to aspire to. I will be different. I will show them another way."

"And what if you fail?" he asked, his voice low, a challenge hidden within. "What will you do when the darkness comes for you? When the corrupt ones rise from the ashes of my fall? What will you become then?"

Adira hesitated. The weight of his words pressed down on her, but she knew this moment was pivotal. She could feel the eyes of the world waiting, not just on her, but on what she would become. Could she lead without falling into the same traps as him? Could she maintain her integrity while holding the reins of power?

The silence between them grew heavy, the echoes of the future pressing in on her mind. Dev stood before her, a living reminder of everything she fought against, yet the embodiment of every fear she had about ruling.

As Adira turned away, leaving Dev to ponder his fate, a strange calm settled over him. His eyes followed her as she moved toward the door, the sound of the crowd outside growing louder. Their voices, full of hope and desperation, clamored for a new beginning.

But Dev couldn't help the bitter smile that curled his lips. So, this is it? he thought, his mind swirling in a mixture of cynicism and amusement. The rebel thinks she can do it differently. She believes she can lead without becoming what I am. That she can bear the weight of the throne without it crushing her. Foolish girl.

A low chuckle escaped him, the sound lost in the echo of the grand hall. The people will cheer for her today. They'll see a symbol of hope, of change. They always do. But they don't know what's coming. They think the worst is behind them because I'm stepping down, but they don't understand the real game is just beginning.

Dev's thoughts grew darker, his mind racing as he considered the twists of fate yet to unfold. A leader born of rebellion. Yes, she's strong, but strength isn't enough. She's been forged in grief, in the fire of loss, but that doesn't make her immune. In fact, it makes her vulnerable. Grief doesn't build rulers—it breaks them. And what happens when that grief turns to anger, to rage?

His eyes narrowed as he imagined the inevitable. What happens when she realizes the same thing I did? That no matter how much you want to believe in the people, they're driven by greed, fear, and selfishness. They'll turn on her the moment she falters, and when they do, she'll have to make a choice. And that choice will define her. She'll either crush them under her heel like I did, or they'll devour her alive.

He paused, letting the twisted satisfaction of that thought roll over him. It's amusing, really, he mused, his internal monologue dripping with sarcasm. She thinks she's above it all. But the throne has a way of stripping away your ideals. It forces you to make decisions no one is ready for. And when the weight of those decisions crashes down on her... well, let's just say I'm curious to see how long she lasts.

His grin widened, a cruel edge to his thoughts now. Maybe she'll become the strong ruler they need—ruthless, unyielding. Or maybe she'll be just another puppet, pulled by invisible strings, until the game swallows her whole. Either way, I've already won. Because whether it's tomorrow or years from now, she'll understand one truth: power never changes hands without blood.

He shifted his gaze to the grand window overlooking the city, where the crowds chanted Adira's name. Let them have their moment of hope. Let them believe they've escaped the cycle. Because I know what happens next. I've seen it before. A rebel becoming a chancellor...

His thoughts trailed off, his mind sinking deeper into the abyss of his cynicism. What's that old saying? The brightest flames burn the fastest. And Adira? She's burning bright now, but I wonder—what happens when the fire dies?

A final laugh rumbled from his chest, barely audible but filled with dark amusement. Enjoy your victory, Adira. The real game starts now. And whether you rise as a great ruler or fall as just another casualty of power, I'll be watching. Always.

CHAPTER 15
The reader must now decide

Does Adira end the cycle by ending Dev's life, ensuring he can never manipulate the world again and solidifying her stance as a force for change? Or does she show mercy, keeping him alive, believing that true transformation can only come by rejecting violence—even against a tyrant?

With the decision hanging in the air, Adira's hand hovered near the blade strapped to her side. Dev's eyes locked onto hers, his fate now intertwined with the choice she must make.

Will she kill him to break the cycle of tyranny, proving that she will not allow the darkness to persist?

Or will she spare him, a gesture that could either set the tone for a new era of mercy and hope—or lead her down a path where mercy becomes weakness, and the cycle continues?

The people will follow her lead, but in the end, it's you—the reader—who must decide.

www.ingramcontent.com/pod-product-compliance
Lightning Source LLC
LaVergne TN
LVHW091110150826
845673LV00002B/769

* 9 7 9 8 8 9 6 1 0 1 2 7 7 *